Saekisan

ILLUSTRATION BY
Hanekoto

Contents

Amane Fujimiya

A student who began living alone when he started high school. He's poor at every type of housework and lives a slovenly life. Has a low opinion of himself and tends to put himself down, but is kind at heart.

Mahiru Shiina

A classmate who lives in the apartment next door to Amane. The most beautiful girl in school; everyone calls her an "angel." Started cooking for Amane because she couldn't overlook his unhealthy lifestyle.

"Welcome back, Master."

The Angel Next Door Spoils Me Rotten

7

Saekisan

ILLUSTRATION BY
Hanekoto

YEN ON

NEW YORK

The Angel Next Door Spoils Me Rotten 7

Saekisan

TRANSLATION BY NICOLE WILDER ✳ COVER ART BY HANEKOTO

OTONARI NO TENSHISAMA NI ITSUNOMANIKA DAMENINGEN NI SARETEITA KEN Vol. 7
Copyright © 2022 Saekisan
Illustration © 2022 Hanekoto
All rights reserved.
Original Japanese edition published in 2022 by SB Creative Corp.
This English edition is published by arrangement with SB Creative Corp., Tokyo in care of Tuttle-Mori Agency, Inc., Tokyo.

English translation © 2024 by Yen Press, LLC

Yen On
150 West 30th Street, 19th Floor
New York, NY 10001

Visit us at yenpress.com ✳ facebook.com/yenpress ✳ twitter.com/yenpress
yenpress.tumblr.com ✳ instagram.com/yenpress

First Yen On Edition: June 2024
Edited by Yen On Editorial: Ivan Liang
Designed by Yen Press Design: Liz Parlett

Yen On is an imprint of Yen Press, LLC.
The Yen On name and logo are trademarks of Yen Press, LLC.

Library of Congress Cataloging-in-Publication Data
Names: Saekisan, author. | Hanekoto, illustrator. | Wilder, Nicole. translator.
Title: The angel next door spoils me rotten / Saekisan ; illustration by Hanekoto ; translation by Nicole Wilder.
Other titles: Otonari no tenshi-sama ni Itsu no ma ni ka dame ningen ni sareteita ken. English
Description: First Yen On edition. | New York : Yen On, 2020– |
Identifiers: LCCN 2020043583 | ISBN 9781975319236 (v. 1 ; trade paperback) |
ISBN 9781975322694 (v. 2 ; trade paperback) |
ISBN 9781975333409 (v. 3 ; trade paperback) |
ISBN 9781975344405 (v. 4 ; trade paperback) |
ISBN 9781975348274 (v. 5 ; trade paperback) |
ISBN 9781975372569 (v. 5.5 ; trade paperback) |
ISBN 9781975372583 (v. 6 ; trade paperback) |
ISBN 9781975379742 (v. 7 ; trade paperback)
Subjects: CYAC: Love—Fiction.
Classification: LCC PZ7.1.S2413 An 2020 | DDC [Fic]—dc23
LC record available at https://lccn.loc.gov/2020043583

ISBNs: 978-1-9753-7974-2 (paperback)
978-1-9753-7975-9 (ebook)

10 9 8 7 6 5 4 3 2 1

LSC-C

Printed in the United States of America

Chapter 1

A New Semester with the Angel

When Amane woke up early to get ready for the first day of the new semester, he was just a little disappointed to find no one lying beside him.

Calling the last day of summer vacation eventful would have been an understatement, but Amane wouldn't say it was all bad. He'd learned a great deal about Mahiru, and he'd even gotten a chance to meet with Mahiru's father, Asahi. It was a relief to finally have a better idea about how the man felt, even if only a little, since Mahiru's father had been wrapped in mystery until now.

The whole experience had only convinced Amane more than ever that he wanted to stay by Mahiru's side and protect her for the rest of his life.

And as far as he could tell, Mahiru wanted the same thing. They hadn't made any definite promises yet, but he wanted to believe that when the time came, she would say yes.

The night before, he had teasingly asked her if she wanted to stay over, but ultimately Mahiru went back to her own apartment.

Amane might have insisted if he had gotten the sense that Mahiru was in danger of being crushed by unbearable anguish, but she had simply looked reassured by Amane's words and had answered him with a fleeting smile that, while a little frail, was far from heartbroken.

...As long as she's not pushing herself too hard.

While he changed into his uniform, Amane recalled how Mahiru had been acting the day before. She had settled down considerably after hearing what he'd had to say. It was a little embarrassing when he thought about how much he meant to Mahiru, but he also knew that she needed something more. Amane grimaced as he wondered what he should do if Mahiru was still feeling out of sorts today.

Just as he finished fastening his belt, he heard the sound of the front door unlocking. It was the first school day after summer vacation, so Mahiru must have gotten ready earlier than usual.

When he stepped out of his bedroom, necktie in hand, Mahiru was there tying her apron on in the doorway to the kitchen.

"Good morning."

Amane was quietly relieved to see Mahiru wearing her usual smile.

"Morning. Did you sleep well?"

"I'm not as upset as you think, Amane. Really, I'm all right. It's all done now."

"Maybe, but how you're feeling about it is a whole other can of worms. Well, I'm sure it'll annoy you if I fuss too much, so just let me know if things get tough. I'm here for you."

"Thank you... I'm counting on you."

He could see in her small smile of embarrassment that she really did feel that way, so Amane gave her a little smile in return and then headed for the vanity to straighten up his outfit.

They ate Mahiru's home-cooked breakfast, and just as they were about to leave the house, Mahiru turned to Amane. "Not forgetting something?" she asked.

Amane had pretty much gotten everything ready ahead of time, so he couldn't think of anything. His bag was packed, and he had even double checked it, so no issue there.

"Not really, I don't think so."

"Really?"

"Why do you sound so skeptical?"

"…You weren't going to leave this behind?" Mahiru asked, sounding exasperated as she held up Amane's school-issued necktie, the one that he had decided to put on after breakfast, since it was so stifling in the heat. As soon as she said it, Amane remembered that he had left it behind on the sink when he'd gone to wash his face.

"Ah." He groaned in spite of himself and heard Mahiru sigh.

"We have the opening ceremony today, so we should look our best."

Chiding him, Mahiru started to drape the necktie around his neck, so Amane crouched down, feeling somewhat sheepish.

Of course, he could have tied it himself, since this was something he had done basically every day prior to summer vacation, but if Mahiru was going to do it for him, he wasn't going to stop her.

He smiled a little as he watched her fasten his necktie with such focus.

…I bet she's going to blush when it dawns on her later.

He was amused that they were acting like a newlywed couple.

Amane was grateful she was doing this for him like it was the natural thing to do, and even more than that, he was glad he would get to see Mahiru looking bashful when she realized it later, so he had no complaints.

As he was gazing down at her diligently fixing his necktie, Mahiru must have sensed something different in the way he was looking at her, and she peered up with questioning eyes.

"Is something the matter?"

"No, nothing. Just thinking about how lucky I am."

"And that's fine, but you can be so absent-minded sometimes, Amane."

"You're not wrong. I guess I get careless because I have you around."

"Honestly. What am I going to do with you?"

Mahiru sounded both exasperated and happy. She finished tying the necktie with a satisfied expression. They were doing this all in the entryway of Amane's apartment, so Mahiru looked just like a wife sending her husband off. But Amane knew that if he said that, she would definitely be embarrassed and not talk to him for a little while, so he kept quiet.

Instead, he stroked Mahiru's head once and then offered her his hand.

"All right, ready to go?"

"Yes."

He smiled when she took his hand without hesitation like she had so many times before. Amane opened the door, carrying her bag for her. Mahiru had tried to carry it herself, but since she did so much for him, he wanted to at least do this for her.

Seeing that Amane wasn't going to give the bag up, Mahiru broke into a happy smile and head-butted his upper arm gently.

"What is it?"

"...Nothing."

"In that case, I guess there's no problem then."

Amane wasn't so thickheaded that he didn't know what she wanted to say, but if Mahiru wasn't going to say any more, he was fine with that.

"Okay, we're off," Amane said to nobody in particular.

Mahiru stared at him for a moment, then quietly repeated his words, "We're off."

©Hanekoto

The thought that Mahiru considered his apartment home made him feel embarrassed and happy, and he felt his face soften into a smile, but Mahiru didn't hound him about it.

Mahiru was also smiling happily, not to mention blushing a little, so she didn't have a leg to stand on. She looked happy, and when Amane squeezed Mahiru's hand again, she squeezed his right back.

Despite it being the beginning of September, the summer heat didn't show any signs of retreating just yet. Though it was morning, the air was hot, and the sun was dazzling.

However, once they arrived at school, as a matter of course they found that the air conditioning was already turned on.

"...Are you *trying* to give us heatstroke with your red-hot love first thing in the morning?"

"What are you talking about?"

After making it to his seat in the classroom, Amane was talking with Mahiru, when for some reason, Itsuki spoke to him with an uncomfortable look on his face.

Every classroom in their school had an AC that could heat or cool, so the temperature outside never bothered them.

"Come on, this...you're flirting like you're trying to show off, man."

"Trying to show off? We were just having a normal conversation."

"Sure, yeah, your conversation was technically all regular school talk, but, like, I'm talking about the vibe. The way you two are around each other, that look in your eyes."

After arriving in the classroom and greeting their classmates, Mahiru and Amane had started reviewing for their post-vacation tests together, but apparently their behavior had come off as flirting.

As far as Amane was concerned, he was very serious about test preparation, so the accusation didn't sit well with him.

"Dude, whenever Miss Shiina is involved, you just start getting sweeter and sweeter without even noticing. You've gotta knock it off. In public, at least."

"I wasn't doing anything. All we even talked about was what the tests were going to cover and then I just quizzed her a little."

"…That's what I'm getting at, Amane."

"I'm not following."

Amane looked at his friend in confusion, but for some reason, he got the same exact reaction.

"Look around you."

When he did as he was told and checked the room, he discovered that he was receiving murderous stares from all the other boys in class. The girls seemed charmed and somewhat jealous. Even Yuuta, Kazuya, and Makoto, who had been chatting among themselves, were now giving him stiff, awkward smiles.

Amane's cheek twitched a little.

"You know how hard it's been for everyone to keep their eyes off the two of you lately?"

"…You and Chitose are literally the same, though."

"Uh, *rude*. We're always flirting on purpose, in the open. That's completely different compared to the married-couple vibes that you and Mahiru give off."

"I'm not sure that's true."

In Amane's opinion, doing it on purpose seemed far more problematic, but apparently the class did not agree.

In reaction to Itsuki's words, Mahiru blushed slightly and looked uncomfortable, so she probably felt self-conscious. Amane wished she had said something earlier.

"…Was I being really obvious?" he asked.

"I don't know what I'd call it," Itsuki replied, "but there's a world of difference in how you act around me for sure… Like, we can tell how infatuated you are just by watching the way you look at her and talk to her."

"…We can't really deny the truth of Mister Akazawa's words," Mahiru admitted.

"That bad?"

Naturally, when they were at school, Amane was careful to not interact with Mahiru like they usually did. But from the way Mahiru was currently looking anywhere else, he knew now that he hadn't done a very good job. He touched his own cheek, wondering if he was really making such a sappy face, but he couldn't really tell.

It was the first day of school after summer break, so after the school assembly was over and each class finished meeting with their home-room teacher, the students were free to go home.

Normally, there would be nothing strange about having class after an assembly, but since they were preparing for tests they'd be taking tomorrow, school was dismissed early.

After homeroom wrapped up and they were finished for the day, Chitose came over to Itsuki's seat and flopped onto the desk, grumbling in wholehearted misery.

"I don't wanna take any tessssssts!"

"You don't? As long as you've been studying regularly, all you need to do is review. And we get to go home earlier than usual, so we can take it easy," Amane replied.

"That's just what honor roll students like you and Mahiru say. Normal people don't like tests! Right, Yuuta?"

"Ah-ha-ha. Well, I guess I understand both sides," Yuuta answered. "I don't have track practice on test days, so that makes me feel a little lonely, but I do get to take it easy and rest, so that's kind of nice. I guess I don't worry too much about the tests themselves."

"Tch, I forgot you were an honor student, too..."

Yuuta actively ran as the ace of the track and field club, and sports wasn't the only thing he was good at. He excelled at studying, and in the class rankings, he placed in the top third.

Chitose wasn't a part of any clubs, but there was a time when she was in track and field as well. She was someone who preferred exercising her body over her brain, and apparently, she didn't do very well on the kinds of tests that demanded a lot of time spent sitting at a desk. She didn't like studying in the first place, which was probably the main reason she struggled.

"Itsuki, everyone's ganging up on me!"

"Not sure what I'm supposed to do about it. You're just going to have to try a bit harder, Chi."

"Itsuki, you traitor! You've been secretly studying all break."

"Of course I have. I'll lose my freedom if my grades are too bad." Itsuki laughed cheerfully.

He said his father had been pestering him to get his grades up.

Itsuki had always been clever and intelligent, but he had a tendency to prioritize Chitose, so he ended up with relatively average grades. That did not sit well with his father.

As Amane was preparing to head home while sympathizing with his friends' various domestic struggles, Mahiru walked over with her bag in hand, looking ready to go.

"Sorry to keep you waiting, I was talking with the teacher..."

"It's fine, I was chatting with Itsuki and Chitose. Well, it was mostly Chitose complaining about our tests tomorrow."

"She's a hopeless case, even for me."

"I've been forsaken!"

"You have to know that it's crazy to try to memorize everything the night before. Some might even say impossible... It begs the question of what you thought that long vacation was for."

At Mahiru's very reasonable remark, Chitose lifted her head and looked at her pleadingly, then flopped down on the desk again.

Mahiru shot Chitose a pitying glance that said *You brought this upon yourself.*

Of course, there was nothing Amane could do about Chitose's studying problems.

But Mahiru, who had delivered the harsh truth despite her concern for her friend, pulled a clear folder out of her bag with an uneasy smile and stealthily handed it to Chitose.

"I thought it might come to this, so I've put together a list of only the most important things that I think are likely to turn up on the tests. I think you can avoid failing with this."

"Mahiru, my angel!"

"Please stop squeezing me so tight…"

Mahiru smiled awkwardly when Chitose jumped to her feet and threw her arms around her.

It was worth mentioning that Amane had also had a hand in the creation of the reference material. He was familiar with the teachers who were writing the tests and had discussed it with Mahiru before helping pick out what was most likely to be covered. Of course, their predictions could be wrong, but even if they misjudged their teachers, they had included some material they knew for certain would be on the tests, so passing grades should still be a possibility.

"Amane helped me make it, so you should thank him as well, not just me, okay?"

"Oh, Lord Amane, I'm ever so grateful. Tell me, which would you prefer: a photo of Mahiru stuffing her face with a crepe so excitedly that she gets whipped cream on her cheek, or a photo of Mahiru with big tears in her eyes watching a horror movie?"

"Chitose?!"

"Ooh, both sound good."

"You too, Amane?!"

Mahiru turned red and her eyebrows shot up at the thought that she had been photographed in secret. Amane laughed.

"Just joking."

"...Really?"

"Well, if I can have them, I will, but—"

There was no real crime in having the pictures themselves, and if he could acquire a few that captured Mahiru's casual cuteness, Amane couldn't be happier.

Mahiru made a disapproving face, but since Chitose was cackling with laughter, her anger already had the perfect target. "Chitose, you dummy!"

"Now, let's all play nice and get along, Mahiru. Amane just forgot himself because he desperately wants pictures of his sweetheart."

"That's one thing—this is another," Mahiru declared, and turned away in a huff.

Both Amane and Chitose laughed, which just made Mahiru pout even harder.

"You got them in the end, didn't you?"

As soon as they got home, Mahiru started sulking.

It sounded like she didn't actually mind the fact that the photos had been taken but wasn't very keen on Amane seeing them.

"Oh? I wonder...," Amane remarked.

She looked at him with daggers in her eyes. "...I'll mix a huge helping of wasabi into your soba broth before I serve it to you, if you're not careful. Enough to make you cry."

"I said sorry! I didn't get them."

She was holding his lunch hostage, so he meekly confessed instead of evading the question.

Since Mahiru seemed uncomfortable with it, he had given up

getting the photos without her permission. Of course, he was planning to have Chitose send them to him if Mahiru ever allowed it.

Mahiru was visibly relieved by Amane's words. "That's good to hear," she answered in a tone that told him she had gotten some of her cheer back. She started tying back her hair in preparation for cooking.

"Do you hate your pictures that much?"

"I—I don't exactly hate them, just…I'm making embarrassing faces in them, and it's awkward… They're not cute at all."

"I doubt that. I think you look great no matter what you're doing."

"…There you go again."

Mahiru turned away in an embarrassed huff. When she finished getting her hair into its bun, she put on her apron and began washing her hands.

Amane intended to help assemble the dishes of condiments and sides, so he started washing his hands beside her, but when he glanced sidelong at Mahiru, he saw her face was slightly red.

"What would you do if Mister Akazawa sent me embarrassing photos of you, Amane?" she asked.

"Mm… Depends on what kind, I guess, but unless they were pictures that you couldn't show in public, I think I'd be okay with it. Although, I can't imagine Itsuki sending anything too terrible or even taking a picture like that in the first place. Plus, I don't remember ever making a fool of myself."

"…Would you let him send a picture of you with cat ears?"

"Like when he put them on me at karaoke? Sure, why not?"

She must have meant a picture from the time when the three boys had gone to karaoke together, and Itsuki had made him wear a pair of cat ears that he'd had with him for some reason. Itsuki and Yuuta had barely been able to hold back their laughter, so Amane remembered taking the ears off immediately, but it was beginning to sound like the moment had been preserved in a stealthy photograph.

Amane wasn't particularly bothered by it, but Mahiru's eyes were downcast, and she seemed uncomfortable.

"...I'm one to talk. Sorry for getting your picture without your permission."

"Itsuki's to blame for that one. Anyway, he must have sent it as soon as he took it. He can buy me a hamburger or something, and we'll call it even."

It was frightening to consider that there might still be other photos lying in wait in Itsuki's collection, but Amane didn't think there was anything too terrible.

As he dried his hands on a soft towel that he had just pulled out, he smiled at Mahiru, who was looking apologetic.

"Come on, you don't need to worry about that. Instead of looking sorry, it'll make me happier if you prepare plenty of little side dishes and condiments."

"...Even wasabi?"

"Balance in all things, please."

He answered with a very serious look on his face, and Mahiru smiled a little, probably feeling relieved, as she spooned up larger-than-usual portions of the preprepared side dishes.

"The tests are tomorrow, but I don't think things are looking much better for her," Amane mumbled as he rubbed his belly in satisfaction after they finished eating their soba noodles.

Amane actually enjoyed studying, and he put in a fair amount of effort on a daily basis, so he wasn't worried at all about the tests themselves. Chitose's grades were much more concerning.

"Yeah, you're probably right. These are the kind of tests where you just have to try your best, so..."

"If Chitose heard you say that I bet she'd whine and say, 'You're only saying that because you're an honor student.'"

"Heh-heh. It's even worse because this time there are some subjects that she really struggles with. I tried so hard to teach her the other day."

I bet Chitose complained the whole time, Amane thought, but he stopped before he spoke the thought aloud and stared at Mahiru, who was so calm, even the day before a round of tests.

"That reminds me, what do you want as your reward this time?"

"Huh, reward?"

"It goes without saying that you're going to take the top slot, so you need some other reward, right? I'll do anything, as long as I'm able."

"Last time I let you lay in my lap for your reward, didn't I? In that case, don't you need a reward too, Amane?"

"My reward will be making you happy."

"...That goes for me, too, so it's not fair to say that."

Mahiru pouted just a little bit and slapped her thighs. With a wry smile, Amane squeezed her hand gently.

"I want to do something for you, so let me give the reward this time."

"Hmm... W-well then, there's something I want."

"Something you want?"

Generally speaking, Mahiru wasn't a very materialistic person, so it was unusual for her to say she wanted something, and especially rare for her to ask Amane for it. He peered into her caramel-colored eyes, and she looked away bashfully.

"...So, in your room, you have a cushion, right?"

"Uh, yeah."

"I want that."

Her request for such an unexpected item made him blink repeatedly in surprise. Mahiru must have been embarrassed, because she squirmed in her seat without even trying to hide her red-hot cheeks.

"I usually use that when I'm sleeping, so it's pretty worn out. Is that all right?"

"It's actually better if it's worn out, I mean…um…listen, your scent calms me down, so…"

"…Mahiru, do you maybe have a thing for smells?"

"I-it's not a fetish or anything! I like you, Amane, so I like the way you smell, and it makes me feel happy, that's all!"

"O-oh."

He got the feeling that she had told him something embarrassing. Somehow it was worse than if she had come right out and said that she liked him. Amane scratched his cheek while he thought about the cushion in his bedroom.

Now that she mentioned it, he realized that whenever Mahiru went into Amane's room, she usually held onto that cushion. He'd assumed it was just because she found it calming to hug something, but maybe she had been holding it precisely because it belonged to Amane.

"You don't have to use a stand-in for me like that."

"It's, well…holding you directly is too exciting."

"Really?"

"Yes, okay?! Come on, you smell nice, and you're warm, and your body is firm and manly… It makes my heart pound so hard. If I just want to relax, it's not helpful to be so focused on you."

Mahiru squeezed the nearest cushion. She seemed aware that she had a tendency to grab pillows whenever anything happened.

She wrapped her arms around the cushion with a loving yet somewhat embarrassed look on her face, like she'd been caught hugging a stuffed animal. Amane chuckled quietly and gently stroked her head.

Chapter 2

Overwhelmed by the Angel's Acting Skills

The tests were over before they knew it.

Amane and Mahiru were prepared, so they cleared the exams with plenty of time and energy to spare. Chitose, on the other hand, looked like a corpse by the time she was finished.

The moment her last test ended, she shouted, "I'm free!" And threw both hands up in the air, crying with joy. "Ugh, I'm exhausted! I made it through okay, thanks to you two!"

"You better wait until the results come back to see if you actually made it or not."

"Don't be such a downer, Amane. I'm filled with the feeling of freedom right now! Mahiru, Mahiru, let's go get tea to celebrate!"

"That's fine with me. Um, Amane—"

"It's all right. I'm going to hang out with Itsuki. You two have fun. If you're going to be late, send me a message and I'll come get you."

Chitose, who looked dead tired from nonstop cramming, had finally regained her cheerful expression. Even Amane wasn't thoughtless enough to rain on their parade. He and Mahiru were going out now, but they respected each other's time, and Amane wasn't one to interfere when she wanted to spend time with friends. More than anything, he wanted her to enjoy herself.

Mahiru seemed relieved by how readily Amane agreed. She smiled shyly and said, "All right, then. I'll take you up on that."

Amane watched Mahiru leave as Chitose immediately dragged her out of the classroom by the hand with a big grin on her face.

Itsuki smiled and slapped Amane on the back. "When did you decide that you were going to hang out with me?"

"Just now," he replied.

They hadn't actually made any plans, but Amane wanted his girlfriend to enjoy herself without hesitation. Itsuki clearly understood because he had played along perfectly.

"Gotcha. Well, anyway, even if I go home, there won't be anyone there, so it's all good with me."

"Oh, and also, you owe me a hamburger, so…"

"For what?"

"Karaoke cat ears."

"Caught me, huh? Miss Shiina must have owned up to it."

Itsuki grinned, not looking the least bit guilty, and Amane slapped him on the back—a little forcefully. "I don't really care, but I wish you'd said something first," he scolded his friend.

He was more surprised than mad. It made him curious when Itsuki had managed to leak the photo to Mahiru. Amane always doted on Mahiru, so as long as it made her happy, he didn't really mind if she collected those kind of photos.

"Sure, I'll make sure to let you know. On that note, I wonder what I should send her next?"

"You're not sorry at all."

Itsuki smirked. He apparently still had plenty of photos of Amane in a folder on his phone. Amane frowned, but decided to let him off with just a light glare.

*   *   *

While Mahiru and Chitose were having their tea at a café, Amane and Itsuki went to a hamburger shop together.

This place was often filled with high schoolers sitting and chatting. Amane and Itsuki could see plenty of other students in uniform from their school and from other schools as well.

After they ordered, picked up their food, and made it to their seats, Amane casually looked around and shrugged.

"Lots of people today."

"There sure are. Seems like we weren't the only ones who had exams today. That's what a buddy from another school told me yesterday."

"That explains it. Everyone looks so relieved."

"Amane, people like you who're relaxed from the start are definitely in the minority... Well, let's leave the exam talk aside and eat before it gets cold."

Itsuki was looking at him with slight exasperation, but he quickly moved on and picked up one of the french fries he had ordered.

Amane followed suit. He unwrapped the burger Itsuki had treated him to and sank his teeth into it. It had a familiar flavor, but compared to Mahiru's cooking, it was somewhat lacking. Of course, for junk food this was fine, but it drove home that Mahiru's cooking really was the best.

"...Amane, considering that you're the one who asked to come here, it looks a lot like you're missing Miss Shiina's cooking."

"No way, that's...well, it's true, but I still think this is pretty good. I just know there's better now. I'm still enjoying this."

"Yeah, yeah. Just get married already."

"When the time comes. We're only sixteen, so we're still too young."

"I wasn't expecting a serious answer! But yeah, that seems about right. I get the same vibe from Miss Shiina, too."

"Shut up. Is that so bad?"

"No, it's honestly kind of a relief. It gives me some encouragement, being around people who are dating and already thinking about marriage."

Itsuki also seemed to be keeping the possibility of a marriage with Chitose in mind, so he and Amane had that in common.

The main difference was whether their parents approved of those plans. Itsuki was still hoping to someday get his father's approval and marry Chitose without a big argument.

"…By the way, how are things going these days at home?"

"No changes there, man. For now, I'm working hard to pull in the grades, so my folks won't complain while I keep pressing the issue. That's all I can really do, so there's not much to tell. What about you? How are things progressing? You went home together, right?"

With a big grin on his face, Itsuki gently kicked Amane with the tip of his shoe, so Amane kicked him right back and sipped his orange juice.

"I have no idea what you're talking about. What *things*?"

"What were you doing over the summer, man…? You spent twenty-four hours a day with your girlfriend. It would be pretty pathetic not to do anything at all."

"We're going at our own pace, you know that."

"So you're saying you kissed, but nothing more yet. There are just no words to describe the purity of this relationship."

His mild tone sounded more amused than exasperated, which kind of ticked off Amane, so he kicked him again for good measure.

"…I've invited her to come over and spend the night. We're not ready for that yet, though."

"I can't believe she hasn't even slept over yet. You took her home to meet your parents, but she still hasn't spent the night. It's honestly incredible."

"Shut up... I don't really... I didn't invite her over because I wanted to make a move or anything... I guess I just want to sleep in the same room."

He would be lying if he said he wasn't interested in doing more, but what he wanted most was wrapping themselves up in the same blanket and peacefully drifting off.

Mahiru seemed to like sleeping by his side, so there was also that. It seemed sleeping together in the same bed would make her happy.

"I wonder what that says about you as a boyfriend, though. It's a little unexpected, but it sounds like Miss Shiina wants to stay over, doesn't she?"

"She's not that assertive about it, but yeah. As you might expect, she's probably got some hang-ups about the idea."

"But it's not like you can even make a move. You give up at the first sign of trouble. It's basically guaranteed that you'd freak out the moment you spotted even a hint of rejection."

"Shut up."

Amane didn't enjoy having his timid personality pointed out to him. Of course, he was fully aware that, viewed from an outside perspective, he was a late bloomer and unassertive, so he couldn't deny it.

"...Well, even if you're not going to push for it, I think that might be okay, too. After all, Miss Shiina is probably trying her best with the advice she gets from Chi."

"Hey man, do something about your girlfriend already. I'm almost dead certain she's teaching Mahiru totally unnecessary stuff."

"Sounds like she's just telling her what she needs to know. You guys are both late bloomers and you're not getting anywhere on your own, that's for sure. Chi's probably giving her some ideas right this second," Itsuki said with a laugh.

Amane frowned and silently hoped that Chitose wasn't planting anything weird in Mahiru's head.

*   *   *

Mahiru got home in the evening without messaging him, so he hadn't gone out to meet her.

He didn't think anything in particular about it. But he couldn't help but comment on the fact that she was acting strange once she got home.

"What sort of ideas did she give you?" he asked her directly. He was certain that Chitose had told her something.

Sitting beside him on the sofa, Mahiru turned her face away stiffly, like a machine that desperately needed oil.

Bull's-eye. He wasn't about to let her slip away, so he slid over close to her and leaned in.

Mahiru tried with all her might to escape. "It's nothing," she insisted.

"It doesn't seem like nothing. Look me in the face and tell me again. You can do that much, can't you?"

He pleaded with Mahiru in a gentle voice, but she didn't look at him.

She had her back turned to him, so he wrapped his arm around her stomach and brought his lips to her ear.

"Mahiru..."

With a long sigh, he gently whispered her name and her whole body trembled.

He knew that Mahiru couldn't handle it when he whispered into her ear, so he was doing this on purpose. It was super effective. When he hugged her tightly, wrapping her in his arms and whispering her name again, her body suddenly relaxed, like she was melting from the inside out.

Mahiru leaned back, propping herself against Amane's chest. When he looked down at her face from above, he saw that her cheeks were completely flushed, and that her tear-filled caramel eyes were looking back at him.

"…That's not fair."

"What is?"

"You can't do that. You know that my ears are my weakness."

"But I don't think your ears are your only weakness, are they?"

He also knew that she couldn't stand to be tickled, but if he went that far, he expected that it would actually make her mad, so he decided better of it.

This time, he would only use his voice, and nothing else, to break Mahiru's silence and find out what he wanted to know.

He smiled a little teasingly, and Mahiru squeezed her lips tightly shut.

It looked like she wanted to avoid telling him at all costs, and she was doing her best to turn her face away while still leaning on Amane. If she was truly uncomfortable, she would have run away, so he assumed that meant she didn't exactly want to leave, but she didn't want to tell him, either.

"Come on, if you don't hurry up and tell me, I'll have to pry it out of you."

"…P-pry?"

For some reason, when he said this, Mahiru, whose face was flushed bright red, looked him in the eyes and then suddenly gained an interest in the floor. She seemed even more embarrassed than before.

He had been joking about tickling her a little bit, but she seemed to have taken it as a threat of sexual harassment.

Mahiru was trembling terribly. Thinking that it wasn't a good idea to tease her too much, he put the palm of his hand on her back and propped her back up. That's when Mahiru turned around to look at him.

The look in her eyes was vaguely gloomy and feverish. Amane felt like groaning for a moment, and he roughly stroked her head.

"I'm just kidding, I'm not going to force it out of you."

"…A joke."

"I wouldn't do anything you're uncomfortable with. If you don't want to tell me, you don't have to, but don't take anything Chitose says too seriously."

At any rate, Chitose had probably been telling Mahiru to become more assertive, but if she became too assertive, Amane was pretty sure he'd absolutely lose it, so he hoped she wouldn't take it too far.

Leaving aside Amane's emotional and physical issues for the moment, they were going to be together for a long time, so he genuinely didn't think there was any need to rush things. He said as much, but Mahiru frowned slightly.

"…What I can tell you is…I've been getting her advice on how to interact with the opposite sex."

"Oh, like what?"

"I—I can't get into details, but…but Chitose's been dating a lot longer than me, so I've been getting her to teach me useful things."

"…I don't think you really need her unsolicited advice."

"I'm the one who will decide whether I need it or not."

He couldn't argue with that, but even so, rather than having Chitose plant strange ideas in Mahiru's head that made her feel awkward and oddly aggressive, Amane would have preferred they take their time and move forward little by little.

Amane shrugged awkwardly, and Mahiru hung her head a little bit.

"…Getting the person you like to like you even more, and thinking about different ways to deepen that relationship…isn't that important?"

Mahiru's dejected tone made him realize that he had made a mistake in the way he'd phrased things. She wanted to become closer with Amane, and that was the reason she had been asking Chitose for advice. Despite that, Amane had been quick to dismiss it. That must have made her sad.

He hadn't intended to hurt Mahiru or make her sad, but it was a fact that Amane's words had wounded her.

He started reaching out his hand in apology, but then something hit his body.

The sudden impact made him lose his balance, and he fell over on the sofa. For some reason, Mahiru leaned over him like she was about to get on top. That was when he realized she was already completely lying on top of him.

She was at an extremely risky angle, so he whipped his head up, trying to find somewhere safe to look and ended up meeting her gaze. Mahiru's eyes, peeking out from behind her hanging bangs, had a somewhat impish look in them.

"...Something you picked up from Chitose?"

"Apparently, I'm not pushy enough."

"So you physically pushed me down, huh? Was that earlier stuff all an act, young lady?"

"No, I really did get sad."

She dropped those words with a hint of a bitter smile, and Amane's heart swelled. Without thinking, he put his arms around Mahiru's back.

With her face buried for the moment in the area near Amane's collarbone, Mahiru made a little muffled sound of protest, but he paid it no mind and hugged his sweet, lovable girlfriend tight.

He felt a growing excitement, since it was impossible to ignore just how soft Mahiru was, and the faint aroma of her shampoo made his heart flutter, but those feelings were overridden by stronger emotions. He treasured her so, so much and felt incredibly lucky to have her.

"Sorry, I shouldn't have said that. I was just...you know, worried that learning things from Chitose would be too intense."

"I—I don't think we've gotten to that stuff; not yet."

"The way you said that worries me a little, but okay... You're free to get suggestions from Chitose if you want to, Mahiru. But for me, I don't think it's as much fun if Chitose gives you all kinds of advice."

"Not as much fun?"

"These are my personal feelings, but...well, I was hoping we could learn things little by little—together. If you're only looking at what's ahead and not appreciating what we're doing right now, that kind of feels wrong somehow."

With a bitter smile, he added, "You can call me a chicken. You wouldn't be wrong." He sighed softly.

Amane could see that Chitose's advice was prompting Mahiru to action, and he knew that Mahiru was doing what she was doing because she loved him from the bottom of her heart. That made him extremely happy.

Even so, he didn't want them to rush into things.

"Sorry for saying something so pathetic. I guess I'm a coward, that's all."

"...No, I can really tell that you love me and that you're being careful... But, um, how do I put this... I also...I don't necessarily want to rush either, but you...um, I wondered if maybe you didn't like that?"

"Didn't like it?"

"...You know, me making you w-wait, and stuff."

He could clearly tell what Mahiru was trying to say while squirming with embarrassment as she clung tightly to him. It made him smile even more bitterly than usual.

But it wasn't directed at Mahiru. No, it was meant for his own impatient self.

Considering his position from an outside perspective, Amane figured that having such a strong reaction to such a minimal thing was evidence of his youth and inexperience, and he tried to calm down a little.

And he figured it probably wasn't the best idea to make Mahiru even more conscious about how close they were at the moment.

"I don't hate it at all. I mean, I am a guy, so I've got all kinds of thoughts in my head, but I don't want to rush you or anything. Besides, it's at least a little scary for you, right?"

"...Yes."

"Then it's fine. We can go at our own pace."

He ruffled her hair, and Mahiru smiled in apparent relief before nuzzling her cheek against Amane's chest.

Honestly, he had a lot of feelings about their current situation, especially the way her body was pressed on top of him. But for Amane, his love for Mahiru always came out on top, so he just gently stroked his girlfriend's back.

"Anyway, do you think I could get you to move soon?"

"Am I heavy?"

"You're not heavy, but...please understand."

He lightly patted her back, implying that he wanted her to consider what he was going through, but Mahiru showed no signs of moving. On the contrary, she pressed against him even harder and looked up at him.

When she noticed him grimacing and pressing his lips together, Mahiru cast her eyes downward bashfully, but she didn't seem ready to pull away.

"Could I stay here like this for just a little while longer?"

"...Suit yourself."

He could have forced her to get off, but Mahiru was pressed

against him because she wanted to be, so he intended to respect her wishes.

Amane resigned himself to his fate, swallowed his joy and embarrassment, and let out a little sigh. He put his hand on Mahiru's head. She seemed very satisfied snuggling against him, and with careful movements, he combed his fingers through her soft hair.

Chapter 3

The Angel's Pleas

The following week, the results of the post-summer break exams were posted.

As expected, Mahiru's name sat at the top of the rankings. She cooly gazed at the list until she felt Amane's eyes on her. She flashed him a faint smile.

It was her angelic smile, which felt a little formal, but Amane could sense the deep affection and trust that was hidden behind her expression.

"Hey, congratulations on first place," he said.

"Thank you very much."

"You keep getting good grades because you always work so hard. It's really impressive."

Despite the fact that she also looked after Amane's needs on a daily basis, Mahiru had taken the top rank and seemed to do it with ease. It was all thanks to her steady efforts and all the knowledge she had cultivated.

Even when she spent time with Amane, she also often worked through study books or looked at flashcards. It was obvious she never cut corners on her studies.

"I should congratulate you, too, Amane. You're fifth this time."

"Thanks a lot. That's partly thanks to you. You're a good teacher."

"Heh-heh, I'm honored to receive such praise. You're quick to pick up on things, so teaching you is fun, Amane."

"Thanks… How'd your regular student do?"

"Her ability to concentrate when she's motivated is striking. But usually, it seems like her lack of confidence does her in."

"That sounds like Chitose, all right."

Chitose had placed roughly in the middle of the pack, so it seemed like their reference material had helped.

Itsuki was in a higher position than usual. He had risen about twenty spots from his usual rank, so clearly he'd been trying harder recently. He was the kind of guy who, even though he seemed very carefree, could always get things done.

"For now, this should give us some peace of mind for a while."

"Once we get home, we should compare test answer sheets and have a review session. I think I missed a few things, so I want to review before the wrong ideas stick."

"Good idea, Amane. You really are a good, hard worker."

"That's because I'm trying to keep up with you."

Fundamentally, Amane felt he couldn't compare to his amazing friends.

Of course, he wasn't as good as Mahiru in academics, and he wasn't athletic like Yuuta, nor did he have Itsuki's natural charisma. He'd been told that he was relatively good-looking, but not handsome enough to be a good match for Mahiru's beauty, which had been polished through tireless effort that enhanced her natural looks.

Amane and Mahiru were together because they both liked each other, but from an outside perspective, their relationship was hard to understand.

To silence those annoying naysayers, and so that he could stand tall beside his partner, Amane was trying to improve in every area. His studies were just one of many.

"Besides, the better my grades are, the better my chances, too."

"For what?"

"For getting a job I want."

Grades weren't everything, but if his grades were good, he had a better chance to go somewhere he could gain the sort of knowledge and experience that he was after. When it came down to it, Amane's parents had always urged him to study and get good grades so that he would have more options.

Once he figured out what he wanted to do in the future, he just had to steadily put in the effort, and if he made a name for himself early on, he would be able to get through life without suffering or regrets.

Amane's parents trusted him to study on his own, so they'd simply told him that his grades could be a key to new opportunities in the future, and that studying now just meant fewer regrets later.

During his middle school years, Amane had sometimes found their admonitions annoying, but now that he was in high school and away from his parents, and now that he had found someone important to him, he was thinking again about how important his efforts were.

"I see. How pragmatic, planning ahead."

"Well, I'm sure it's the same for you, too, Mahiru. Plus, I want to become the kind of man that you can depend on."

"Wh-what?"

"Well, it wouldn't feel right to be supported emotionally *and* financially. We should support each other. I can't just depend on you for everything."

Amane felt like Mahiru provided almost everything for him in their daily lives. If she ever had to support him financially as well, it would tear apart whatever tiny bit of pride he had left.

If possible, he wanted to earn enough to provide for Mahiru and still have some left over.

Mahiru seemed to understand what Amane was trying to say. Her cheeks flushed slightly, and she answered awkwardly, saying, "I-is that right?" Which made Amane smile.

"My partner is too amazing, so it gives me a reason to work hard."

"Uh, s-sorry...?"

"No, no, I want you to be just the way you are. This is something that I'm working on by myself."

"...All right, then I'll be cheering you on." Then she smiled, said, "But first, our review session...," and lightly grabbed Amane's sleeve before going back into the classroom together.

"That reminds me, you wanted that cushion for your reward, right?"

Once they were home and working on their review session after dinner, Amane remembered the earlier request.

Mahiru had been sitting beside him explaining the test questions that Amane had missed, but at the mention of the reward, her eyes shifted around a little.

"...Well, um, I do want it."

"Okay, if that's all you want, consider it yours."

"Th-that and, um, something else..."

"Is there anything else that you want?"

"Well, I w-want...um..."

For some reason, Mahiru was having an extremely difficult time saying it. Amane gently stroked her head, trying to help her calm down.

For once, Mahiru, who was basically never selfish, had something she desired, and he wanted to make sure she got it.

She briefly gave him a soft smile after he patted her, but then immediately stared at the floor bashfully.

"So, I... I want you to k-kiss me."

"Kiss?"

It wasn't like they kissed constantly, but on the other hand, it wasn't like they had never kissed before, either. They both did it casually, whenever they felt like it. Sure, it could be seen as a kind of reward, but Amane felt like it was more of an everyday thing, rather than a special request for ranking first on the exams.

Although he wasn't sure whether something so minor really counted, if it was what Mahiru wanted, he was happy to oblige.

"…As you wish."

He whispered as softly as he could, with a slight chuckle riding on his breath, then slowly, so as not to startle her, he brought his lips to hers.

Mahiru's entire existence was soft and gentle.

Her lips were no exception. They were lush and tender and perfect.

The faint sweetness that he sensed on top of all that must have been the natural perfume of Mahiru's body.

As he pecked lightly at her light-pink lips, he indulged in the moment.

Her body was trembling timidly the whole time Amane's lips were caressing and devouring hers, but she didn't pull away or seem to hate it, so he could only assume that she was happy.

…*She's so cute*, he thought.

As he was kissing her, he looked at Mahiru's face. She looked embarrassed but also pleased. He could see right away it wasn't a bad reaction.

Though she tended to embarrass easily, she seemed to like kissing, so Amane didn't feel like he needed to hold back.

As he might have expected, Mahiru's body jolted when he first tasted her lips, but soon both her lips and her body slackened.

With her body and facial expression soft and relaxed, Mahiru looked adorable, and he pecked at her lips again.

©Hanekoto

It was a clumsy make out session, and he held himself back, giving her only very light kisses. But even that much was enough to fill Amane with passion and love welling up from deep inside him, enough to drive him crazy. The desire for more started to slip through the cracks of his wall of reason, which had started to crumble bit by bit the more he tasted Mahiru.

As he was savoring Mahiru's lips to the fullest, she started tapping on his chest like she wanted something.

It wasn't a gesture of discomfort, and she didn't look like she was at her limit, so Amane reasoned that she was simply telling him she had had enough, and he slowly pulled his lips away from hers. With red cheeks, Mahiru peered up at him.

"...Oh, no. I d-didn't want you to stop in the middle..."

"That wasn't a signal to stop just now?"

"N-no, it wasn't...um, so, the next kind of kiss, you know..."

Her words, which came out in a thin voice which could not have been more faltering or bashful, eventually helped Amane belatedly understand what she had been asking for, and he let out a little groan.

The kiss that Mahiru had been hoping for involved more than simply touching lips. It was the kind of kiss for people who wanted a deeper connection with their lover. That was why she hadn't seemed displeased when he'd sucked on her lip as he kissed her. In fact, she had actually relaxed her mouth a little.

Amane couldn't believe she wanted that, and his feelings must have been very apparent because she blushed deeper red and stared at the floor.

"I-it's shameful, I know that. But I also...want to kiss you back, and to know you...more deeply."

"O-oh...that's... Until now, I thought you weren't up for...stuff like that..."

"…I got embarrassed, hearing people talk about it, but…if it's with you…"

Hearing her say something so charming and courageous was so hot that Amane thought he was going to burst into flames on the spot.

Plus, Mahiru was so flushed, it seemed like she was feeling the same heat. Perhaps because she had said her true desires out loud, she was trembling with nervousness and shame. And yet, when she glanced up at Amane, there was faint but unmistakable anticipation in her eyes.

He once again focused his gaze on the glossy luster of her lips, the same lips he had been relishing just a moment earlier. They were now casually parted, and Amane let his lips close in on them again.

Mahiru made a small noise in her throat, and a bewildered expression crossed her face, but that almost immediately dissolved.

Telling himself that he could only go a little bit further and that he had to stay calm, Amane matched Mahiru's pace and slowly, very slowly, allowed himself to savor Mahiru's passion.

If he let his self-control slip now, he would only want more and more, with no end in sight, so stopping after just a little making out was the right decision as far as Amane was concerned.

His heart was thumping so hard he could hear it loud and clear. He hadn't expected just a few minutes of kissing to affect his body and heart so fiercely.

The enraptured look in Mahiru's eyes showed faint disappointment when he pulled his lips away…and Amane, who couldn't look directly at her for a number of reasons, instead embraced Mahiru and buried his face in the nape of her neck.

"…Don't look like you want it so badly, please. You'll kill me."

"I—I didn't…think I…"

"You really did… Did I grant your wish?"

When he whispered into her ear, he felt her body tense, but Mahiru immediately hugged Amane back and answered quietly, "Yes."

Amane wasn't sure what he would have done at that point if she had asked him for more. It probably would have annihilated any reservations he still had.

...That was a close one.

And the danger hadn't passed. He had forcefully embraced Mahiru and brought his lips to her neck, but he couldn't help but feel that he had gone ahead and poured fuel onto the fire himself. He'd positioned himself right next to her slender, fragrant, milky white neck, and there was no way he could not react.

Mentally chiding himself for his foolishness at dangling bait before his own eyes, he slowly lifted his head and saw Mahiru there, who for some reason was flushed an even darker red than before.

"Th-that spot's too...t-ticklish, or actually—"

"...Mahiru, your neck and ears are really sensitive, huh?"

Her reaction was adorable, which was bad news for him, he thought, as he buried his face in her neck once again and faintly traced its curve with his lips. She jolted and shrieked in a sweet voice.

When Mahiru moved, a gently sweet, but not too sweet, fragrance tickled his nose, as if some of it had spilled from her voice and into the air.

The scent threatened to disarm his sense of reason. Amane was finding it incredibly hard to pull away from Mahiru, so he simply stayed there enjoying that scent and her warmth and tenderness.

"You smell so good."

"That's...it's because I put on lotion after I take my bath. To moisturize. That must be it."

He'd thought that she was giving off that nice scent because it seemed like she had taken a bath before coming over that day, but apparently it was the fragrance of her body lotion.

However, he was almost sure that Mahiru had her own unique scent apart from the lotion.

His girlfriend, who had a lightly sweet fragrance to her, even if she didn't do anything, really devoted herself to her grooming and was meticulous about taking care of her skin.

"Is it even possible to have smoother, more delicate skin than you, Mahiru?"

"I don't just smear skin products on, you know. I protect it by being careful about all sorts of other things."

"Being a girl sounds hard... I'm impressed you can put that much effort in."

"...Well I do it, um, for my own benefit, so..."

"Yeah, I guess that's true. You do like self-improvement, and girls like to make themselves look good, after all."

Mahiru had seemingly always enjoyed dre   . Amane was sure that she would still pay very close atter   ner appearance, even if they weren't dating.

Amane had never been under the delusion that girls made themselves look good for the sake of boys. He believed Mahiru when she said that she did what she did for her own benefit.

But it seemed like that wasn't all Mahiru had to say. "...There's also...something more," she replied quietly.

"More? You mean there's another reason?"

"...I mean, um...isn't it nice when it feels nice to the touch?"

"Well, it is your body, so yeah, that makes sense."

The owner of the body was the one who touched it the most, so they could appreciate that the most.

"Th-that's not... I mean when you touch me."

Because he had had the exact same thought, Amane made a foolish noise of surprise when Mahiru said this.

"I would hate it if I was all dry and rough, and you were

disappointed when you touched me, Amane, and…isn't it nicer for the person doing the touching if I'm smooth and soft?"

"S-sure it is."

Amane had never considered that Mahiru thought about him touching her when she moisturized, and he was clearly flustered by the idea.

Mahiru, for her part, was bright-red in the face, but she didn't seem like she was going to take the words back. She was trembling and shaking as she hugged him even more tightly.

"D-don't misunderstand me, please. About it being for your sake, or for my own sake… It's just, I want you to touch me a lot. That's my request."

"…You want me to…touch you?"

"…Being touched…feels nice, and it makes me happy. It only makes sense, I guess, that I would put in the work so you would touch me and want me."

Her words, which came out in an excited voice full of hesitation and shyness, were more than enough to loosen the reins of reason that had been holding Amane in check.

He felt that he could hear a quiet, distant voice telling him to stop, but he understood best of all how powerless it was. Otherwise, he wouldn't be touching Mahiru like he was.

Mahiru was smiling a gentle, bashful smile, and when he covered her lips, a purring sound escaped from the gap between them.

As if to suck up that sound, he parted his own lips, and slipped his tongue into her mouth. Mahiru's voice hoarsened, becoming a small, sweet thing.

Even though the two of them had kissed like this for the first time just a moment earlier, somehow Amane naturally started to devour Mahiru, probing her mouth deeper and deeper.

His giddy mind was spinning, either because he was so enthralled with Mahiru that he wasn't coming up for air, or because his instincts were pushing him onward, intensifying his urges and trying to melt away every safeguard.

Either way, the puddle of goo that used to be Amane's brain decided that he should enjoy Mahiru even more, and from where she was in his arms, he pushed her down so that she was under him.

Once she was lying down flat on the sofa, Mahiru focused her gaze desperately on Amane, her teary eyes looking like she didn't know what was going on. Amane, without answering the question that her eyes were asking, dove into her soft lips once again.

She either didn't have the willpower to resist him, or wasn't planning to resist him anyway, or perhaps simply didn't know what to do.

Mahiru, who was letting it happen, reached with her hand, searching for something to cling to.

When he gripped her squirming hand, pressing their palms together, all the stiffness in her body relaxed, as if she were reassured by the gesture.

Actually, it was probably more accurate to say that she had gone limp, unsure of what to do now that Amane had her at his mercy.

Yet her gestures told him that she trusted him, and he got the sense that he was allowed to continue.

He showered Mahiru with an abundance of loving and passionate feelings that rushed up from deep inside him, then gulped down all the feelings that came flowing out of her. After fully enjoying Mahiru's incredible sweetness, he slowly pulled his lips away.

Taking a series of short, ragged breaths, he looked down at Mahiru, who was peering up at him with a dazed look that was both saccharine and slack.

"...Are you still...willing to...let me keep going?"

He traced his finger along her neck as he asked, as gently as he possibly could, and he felt Mahiru's body jolt. Her eyes roamed around the room, not ever fully meeting his gaze.

Amane, who had just barely come back to his senses, looked down at Mahiru directly, as he suppressed the urges and passions that were still welling up out of him.

He gently released Mahiru's hand and let their fingers slip apart as he sat up. He knew that if he continued pinning her down any longer, he wouldn't be able to hold himself back.

"...I don't have as much restraint as you think I do, Mahiru. I'm doing my best to hold out here, and this is how I behave."

Even though he wanted to treasure her, all it had taken was the slightest push from his desires and urges for him to get so carried away. He felt keenly and clearly that he was a man, and those feelings came with a slight sense that he was somehow horrible.

"I think that...probably wasn't what you had in mind, Mahiru. You just wanted me to touch you, you just wanted to sink into that happy feeling. I'm the one who brought our bodies into the equation."

Amane loved Mahiru from the bottom of his heart. He wanted to treasure her and make her happy.

It was precisely because he felt that way, that even when he put his hands on her, he did everything he could to hold himself back, although he knew she didn't dislike it. He had never pinned her down before, even when they had been getting close in his bed.

And yet, with a single word from Mahiru, he had forgotten all about the danger and just thought about getting as much of her as possible.

"I'm sorry for suddenly forcing things."

"Why...do you assume that I didn't like it...?"

Out of guilt, Amane averted his eyes a little bit. Her trembling voice reached out to him.

"It, um, I didn't dislike it, not even a little. I was surprised and really excited, but…I'm not mad at you, I'm not rejecting you, and I don't hate you for it."

"You weren't scared?"

"Not scared, exactly, but I'd say it was probably a little too sudden and that caught me by surprise. I mean, this is…it's the first time you've been so forward, Amane."

Then he looked Mahiru in the face again, and saw her looking back at him, red all the way out to her ears, but it definitely wasn't disgust or rejection. In her eyes, he saw embarrassment, mixed with a little bit of…anticipation.

"I was wondering who you were, suddenly, kissing me like that."

"…Uh."

"So don't make such a regretful face, please… The thing is, I was happy to see just how much you love me. B-but next time, um, give me a little more…more time to prepare myself. And please, do it in a way that's not so intense."

She didn't say she disliked the kiss; in fact, she seemed ready to accept the next one. In spite of himself, Amane's face contorted with emotion.

"Mahiru, I'm sor—"

"If you apologize again, I'll get mad."

"…Thank you."

"That's better."

He thanked her meekly, and she looked back at him with an amused smile that seemed to say *You're hopeless*, and pressed her lips together.

In the end, everything was all right because Mahiru was so tolerant, but Amane felt that if it had been anyone else, she probably would have despised him.

Feeling a little disappointed in himself for his lack of self-control, and relieved that Mahiru was so kind and loving, Amane gently stroked Mahiru, who seemed to have calmed down.

It was overwhelming how much he adored Mahiru, who had a happy look on her face, but he had almost forced her into something a short while ago, so he couldn't kiss her with any pressure. Instead he restricted himself to simply gently and politely touching her.

"Amane, you're awfully easy to read."

"Huh?"

"I can see that you're being careful so that you don't overdo it this time."

"There's nothing else I can do... If I overdo it, I might not hold back."

"Amane. If I really don't like something, I can stop you, physically, from going too far."

"...Don't remind me."

Amane cracked a smile, thinking back to an exchange they'd shared when he'd decided to start having dinner with Mahiru, and she also smiled in amusement.

"Heh-heh. So you can relax, okay?"

"I wonder if I can... Mahiru, you don't generally hate the things I do, right?"

"Uh-oh, you found me out. But it's because you always adjust to match me, you know? You're incapable of putting yourself first, Amane."

Laughing elegantly, Mahiru sat up and quietly touched Amane's cheek. She was wearing a gentle smile. There was no sign of her earlier confusion or bewilderment.

"...Well, as far as I'm concerned...I want to do it again. Properly."

Her voice trailed off at the end, sounding even more embarrassed as it did, probably because she was feeling shy about her request.

Amane's face immediately flushed at the word *again*, but Mahiru was looking at him with eyes full of expectation, so he took her lips so naturally that he surprised even himself.

This time, Mahiru accepted it, wrapping her arms around Amane's back.

Earlier, he had followed his urges and kissed her deeply, but this time he touched Mahiru gently, trying to soothe her, because he got the feeling she was a little withdrawn and embarrassed.

He poured his love into his kisses, and they made Mahiru melt even more than before. The beguiling, sweet sounds that spilled faintly from her mouth were Amane's alone.

The more he thought about that, the more he loved her. He proceeded slowly, desperately holding himself in check so that he didn't devour her all at once as the two of them shared their passion together. It was like they were melting into each other completely. As he kept on kissing her, he felt euphoric that Mahiru was responding to him even a little.

After they'd been at it for a while, he felt a tap on his back that meant she was at her limit.

If they went on for too long, even Mahiru would start to have problems, so he reluctantly pulled away and looked down at her. There was a steamy smile on her face and her breaths were coming hard. He spotted tears in her eyes, but she quickly lowered her gaze to escape from his sight.

"A-any more than this is…um, I'm at my limit, in more ways than one, so we can't do any more today."

"Okay."

"…But that…was fun. I'm happy. I think I got a little too much of a reward, huh?" Mahiru mumbled, bashful and awkward.

Overcome with love, Amane didn't kiss her anymore, but instead embraced her again, unwilling to separate from her slender body.

Chapter 4

The Culture Festival Brings a Premonition of Trouble

Once they made it through the midterm exams, the next event on the horizon was the big yearly exhibition that was the culture festival.

The school that Amane and his friends attended put a lot of work into events like this and the whole student body participated, so the budget for each class was large, and the students tended to plan elaborate projects every year.

"All right, so let's decide on our class project, whoo-hoo!"

Of course, they had to decide as a class what they would be doing for the festival, so when the time came, everyone naturally got excited about it.

Itsuki was standing up at the teacher's lectern, obviously in high spirits.

Everyone had known that Itsuki, who loved festivals, would stand as a candidate for the culture festival committee, but Amane had to laugh at the fact that he had actually gotten the position.

Itsuki was completely in his element, lively and animated, gesturing at the blackboard with a pointer that he had brought himself as he indicated the list of ideas written there in large characters.

"Let's see, when it comes to culture festival exhibits, the most important thing to note is that the number of food stands per grade is limited. And since basically every class is going to propose some sort of café, if that's what we want to do, we should prepare for wildly fierce competition."

It was only reasonable that there was a limit on the number of classes that could serve food.

When the students ran them well, stands that served food were always very popular. But if the school didn't manage things carefully, they could end up with a situation where almost every class wanted to run one.

If that happened, the festival would be nothing but food and drink, without variety, so a limit had been set. In addition to that limit, they had to keep in mind how much room and time the cooking facilities could support, as well as rules about sanitation. Essentially, there was no way that every request could be granted.

"Next up, our budget and the school equipment that we can use are listed on the sheets I handed out, so take a look at those. Even if something's not written there, if we want to buy it, I can check on each item. For now, give me ideas that are likely to stay within the budget… Come on then, anyone who has a project they want to do, raise your hand."

Several classmates shot their hands up in response to Itsuki's instruction, scrambling to be first.

Everyone's eyes blazed with excitement. This was a major event, something to really look forward to, and something they considered important.

Well, I got by without trying too hard last year, but…

Amane, who lacked the energy and enthusiasm of the typical student, had always managed to slack off, even during the culture festival.

He was the type who preferred things like booths selling homemade goods, where all he had to do was make his items as instructed and tend to the storefront when it was his turn.

And so he watched the others get excited, almost like he was observing them from afar.

"Over here! Obviously, I think we should do a classic café!"

"Oh, sure, I expected that would come up. So you mean an ordinary café?"

"How about a maid café?"

"I mean, we've got Miss Shiina in our class, so…it would definitely be a hit."

Someone added that last comment quietly, and all their classmates glanced over at Mahiru. Amane didn't find this amusing in the least, but he couldn't say anything. It would have been childish for him to complain, so instead of speaking up, he decided to wait and see how things went.

"Ha-ha-ha, I feel like you're not thinking about the budget at all, but I like the spirit! Okay, for now, let's put that down as a possibility."

As Amane was shooting unamused glances at the boys who got excited at the mention of Mahiru in a maid outfit, he made eye contact with Itsuki. The look in Itsuki's eyes asked him if he was okay with it. Amane replied with a sour face.

If he had to say whether it was good or bad, well, he would have to say that it was bad.

Even under normal circumstances, Mahiru always stood out, and some treated her as a kind of spectacle. And recently, people had been saying that she looked even more adorable, so if they made Mahiru wear a maid's outfit, the students were sure to swarm around her, even though she would probably have a hard time dealing with it.

On the other hand, the merit of the plan was that sales were

©Hanekoto

practically guaranteed. Mahiru's presence would be foolproof advertising, and there was no doubt that the boys would pile into their classroom just to get a glimpse of her.

Mahiru herself put on an indescribably awkward smile once she became the topic of discussion. Amane wasn't surprised. He imagined it didn't feel good to be put on display like that.

But in the end, it was only one proposal, and it wasn't like he could shoot it down as soon as someone mentioned it. If Mahiru really hated the idea, Amane would have no choice but to block it from happening.

"Well, a maid café might be something that interests all the guys, but try to remember the budget as you make your suggestions. Okay, next idea?"

At Itsuki's urging, people brought up all the standard suggestions, like a haunted house, or selling curry or udon noodles, and the blackboard quickly filled with white writing.

But everyone's…or mostly the boys' interest, seemed to stay with the maid café, and Amane could hear people whispering about it.

"Still, Miss Shiina in a maid's outfit…"

"Wait, but that guy, Fujimiya, is here, so…"

"Nah, Fujimiya's a man, too. He must want to see his girl dressed as a maid."

He could hear them, but unfortunately for them, he wasn't in favor of the idea.

He would be lying if he said he had absolutely no desire to see it, but that didn't mean he wanted to show her off. He knew it would tire Mahiru out, so he really didn't want to let them continue down that path.

As he looked in their direction, he shot the boys a piercing look, and they must have noticed his gaze, because they hurried to avert their eyes.

Mahiru must have seen it. She smiled slightly, so Amane let up on glaring at the other boys.

"All right then, Amane, any suggestions?"

Suddenly Itsuki called out to him, and Amane looked at Itsuki without bothering to hide his sour expression.

"Why me?"

"Because you looked like you had something to say."

He did, though not to Itsuki. But now that he had been called by name and everyone's eyes were on him, it would spoil the atmosphere if he didn't say anything.

Wondering what to do, he suggested out loud the thing that seemed the most enjoyable.

"If I have to make a suggestion, then I'd probably go for researching a part of local history and presenting our findings or something like that. I think that could be good."

The class fell silent at Amane's suggestion, proving it was not what they wanted to hear.

It was like he had thrown cold water on all their excitement. The atmosphere in the room was extremely uncomfortable.

"Man, who cares about that?" someone remarked.

"You're gonna make a deliberately super-serious suggestion when we're all having fun?" another student replied.

"But I think it's actually a pretty good idea," Amane argued. "If we're doing a presentation, then all we have to do during the prep phase is research and get our materials together, right? If we can do that, and have a few people take turns manning the presentation area while the culture festival is going on, then everyone else is free. Sure, we won't really get the feeling that comes with hosting a whole attraction as a class, but we'll get to have tons of fun at the festival itself, won't we? We won't have to worry about the time and can see as much as we like of the other classes' stalls."

Once he put it that way, he heard murmurs of understanding throughout the classroom.

Frankly, Amane was perfectly aware that a presentation on local history at the biggest event of the year didn't hold much interest for the students. They all knew that there had been important developments in the history of their area, but without a doubt, people would question why they were choosing to present it at this event.

It wasn't really the sort of thing that classes went out of their way to do for the culture festival, which was a unique opportunity for the students for going a little wild. But Amane's real objective in suggesting it was the freedom it afforded them after they were finished.

Cafés were popular, but they took a lot of effort, and the class would have to spend a long time working on the day of the festival.

Since they would be handling money, they'd have to be very careful running a café, and if any problems arose, they would cause serious problems both in and out of school. It would be an incredible amount of work.

If they did some sort of presentation instead, since the culture festival went on for two days, each student would probably not even have to work for a full hour. It was extremely good return on their time and labor.

A big reason he was in favor of this plan was that unlike with a café or shop, no money would change hands on the day of the festival, so all they had to do was stand around, carefree.

On top of that, it would be way less anxiety-inducing for their classmates who had no confidence in their ability to serve customers, or in their looks, or their cooking abilities. Amane counted himself among their number.

"I don't know how to tell you, but that's the most Amane thing I've ever heard."

Itsuki didn't hide his amusement, but Amane had made his

suggestion and that's all there was to it, so he turned away and closed his mouth.

Mahiru was also looking at him like she wasn't surprised, so that was uncomfortable. It wasn't like he could take the words back, so he just let it go with a quiet sigh.

"Uh, all right, so the maid café has the most votes. We've settled on a maid café, then. Is that okay?"

In the end, the class tentatively voted to host a maid café. The option certainly got the most male votes.

"But listen, now I'm going to tell the student council about our choice, and then they're probably going to draw lots, so if we don't win that lottery, we'll go with our second choice, the haunted house. Also, when it comes to costumes, that's definitely not something we can prepare and still stay within budget, so we'll be looking to use any connections we can. If anyone has any idea how to make that happen, go ahead and call in some favors. If we can't find any costumes, we'll go with a regular café instead, so be prepared for that possibility."

Itsuki had been entrusted with leading the project, and he concisely rattled off all the rules and requirements with his characteristic cheerfulness, then left the classroom, presumably to go report to the student council.

The air in the classroom relaxed into an excited commotion. Amane let out a little sigh and put his chin in his hands, then sensed Mahiru approaching.

"What are we going to do?" he moaned.

"What will we do...? There's nothing we can do about something that's already been decided," Mahiru said, wearing a strained smile.

Even if that was true, Amane still felt kind of irritated about it.

"If you don't want to do it, you have to tell them straight away."

"I'm not necessarily opposed, but…um, are you not a fan of maid outfits, Amane?"

"I don't really like them or dislike them. But I do think you would look good in one. Your apron always looks great on you."

"O-oh really…? Okay, I'll do my best."

"No, you don't have to force yourself—"

"If it'll make you happy, I'll wear the outfit."

When Mahiru flashed him a beautiful smile, he saw the other boys behind her quietly, but triumphantly, celebrating. It was all Amane could do to keep his face from twitching.

"Fujimiya, you look like you're in a pretty bad mood."

Once Yuuta pointed it out, Amane realized for the first time that his feelings were clearly visible on his face. Yuuta was taking advantage of the fact that he had a rare break from club practice after school to hang out.

"…Is it that obvious?" Amane asked.

"Oh, no, I think you look basically the same as always. I just somehow got the feeling, that's all."

Amane had been about to leave to buy some reference books at the bookstore attached to the station when Yuuta caught up with him. Thinking about what his friend said, Amane unconsciously touched his own cheeks. He felt like his face was stiffer than usual, and that he had more of a wrinkle in his brow.

He had been trying not to let it show too much, but he hadn't been able to completely control it. A mixture of embarrassment and shame welled up inside him, eliciting a heavy sigh.

"Well it's…I dunno—it's not a good feeling. I don't like the thought of my girlfriend being on display. If I could, I'd like to keep her to myself."

He thought it was natural to think that way. Amane wasn't exactly happy a mass of people would be ogling the girl he adored. Curious gazes were one thing, but he was especially bothered by the people who would be looking at her *that* way.

"At the same time, it's not like Mahiru hates the idea, and it would just be immature of me to raise objections and demand special treatment for my girlfriend when the class decided this together, so I guess I've got no choice but to keep quiet. I know that Mahiru will get part of the proceeds. It just seems like she's taking on a lot and not getting much in return, and that bothers me."

"Dang. Sorry, man."

"You didn't do anything wrong, Kadowaki. I'm to blame for not selling my plan better to the class."

There wasn't the slightest need for Yuuta to apologize. That said, Amane couldn't exactly blame the classmate who had suggested the café, so he had some unresolved feelings just sitting on his chest.

Amane sighed heavily, feeling helpless since it had already been decided, and Yuuta also put on an awkward smile.

"I voted for the presentation, for what it's worth. It was realistic and our best option for low-work, high-fun. That, and I think they're probably going to send me out to serve customers..."

"Yeah."

If Mahiru, renowned as the most beautiful girl in school, was going to serve customers, then naturally, Kadowaki would also be working the floor since he was also very popular with all the girls.

Yuuta himself sounded like he would prefer to work behind the scenes, but that probably wasn't going to happen. At times like these, those who possessed exceptional beauty were at something of a disadvantage.

"...The boys aren't going to wear maid costumes, too, right?"

"Of course I'd like to believe that that's not going to happen...

If the girls are in maid outfits, the boys will probably dress up like butlers to match them, right? If someone comes through with the costumes, that is."

"Ah, about that, well…some of the girls in our class apparently know someone who runs that kind of café…and they can get us costumes for both the guys and girls, I heard."

"Oh no…"

This was the worst possible news for Amane, who had been brainstorming ways he could prevent them from getting maid clothes.

Now that they had a clear path to the costumes, it was almost certain Mahiru would be wearing one and waiting tables.

If there was a silver lining, it was that it sounded like they were going to get someone to prepare separate outfits for the boys, so they wouldn't be forced into a cross-dressing disaster.

"I can't believe this is the kind of thing that brings our class together in solidarity… But even if some of the other boys get dressed up and serve customers, you're going to have a hard time, Kadowaki."

The attention of all the girls was sure to concentrate on Yuuta. It seemed like it was quite a hardship.

"I don't know why you're talking like this is someone else's problem. I think you're going to get recruited, too, Fujimiya."

"Huh?"

"You can cook, right?"

"…I wouldn't say I can't cook, but I'm definitely not great at it, either."

Amane wasn't incapable of cooking, but he didn't have the skill to make something that was good enough that people would be happy to pay for it. He had no trouble making things he ate on a regular basis, and he could cook well enough to avoid being judged too harshly by Mahiru, but that was about it.

Compared to before, he had made quite a bit of progress, but he was reluctant to offer anything he made for sale.

"Then I think you'll either be in the kitchen, or get sent out to wait tables… If you're working in the back, then you'll still be close by, but you won't be able to see how things are going with Miss Shiina, and that'll probably bother you. You wouldn't like it if some weirdo laid eyes on her, right?"

"Well, that's true, but…who would I be dressing up for?"

Once he considered being able to keep an eye on Mahiru, in case some rude individual laid a hand on her, serving customers seemed like the better option.

If Mahiru was wearing a maid costume, then Amane didn't mind swallowing his shame and wearing similar attire. But he couldn't help feeling like it would be a waste to put him in something smart like a butler's attire.

"For Miss Shiina, I suppose. It seems like it would make her happy."

"Okay, that's fair."

"Also, haven't you started turning heads ever since your makeover, Fujimiya?"

"I don't know about that."

"Probably because you only have eyes for Miss Shiina."

He felt awkward hearing Yuuta say that.

It was true he focused on Mahiru a lot, so he hadn't noticed any new looks or anything from the other girls. He never expected anyone to be looking at him in that way to begin with, so he had no idea.

He looked at Yuuta in disbelief, but Yuuta shrugged and said, "You just don't realize how you come off." So Amane had no reason to think he was lying.

"Once in a while, you ought to pay attention to the way people are looking at you, Fujimiya. Well, in our class, the only looks you get are looks of amusement, so there's no danger there, I think."

"That doesn't really make me happy, either."

"It's your fault for flirting with Miss Shiina all the time."

"...We're not doing it out in the open."

"Ah-ha-ha!"

Yuuta grinned, but didn't seem to believe him. Amane grimaced slightly.

"Well, who's it hurting anyway? Amusing people is way better than getting harassed for it. I wouldn't want you to end up like Miss Shirakawa once did."

"...You mean the thing about the love rival?"

When Yuuta brought it up in a slightly solemn tone of voice, Amane joined him in frowning.

They would never mention it around the couple, but Amane had heard that his best friend Itsuki and his girlfriend Chitose had to overcome a lot before they started dating.

It was hard to imagine now, but Chitose had apparently given Itsuki the cold shoulder when she first met him. Back then, she hadn't sugarcoated her feelings.

Chitose had been outstanding as a track and field athlete, but a fight had broken out between her and an upperclassman on the team over Itsuki, ultimately forcing her to quit the club.

She hadn't wanted to admit that an upperclassman in her club was jealous of her talent and harassing her, but she had also known that the other girl was capable of anything. And she must've known that if the boy that upperclassman liked started to approach her instead, the harassment would only get worse. She'd had to do something.

"Right. Ultimately it caused a lot of trouble, and she had to quit track, you know. I really hate that kind of bullying, so...I'm relieved that people have accepted you as a couple."

Yuuta had watched Itsuki and Chitose have a rough time, so that was probably why he was so worried about Amane and Mahiru.

"...Yeah."

"So go ahead and show off what a good couple you are at the culture festival, just like you always do. Flirt so much that no one will even consider taking her away from you."

"I'm not trying to make a show of it."

"Ha-ha, that's a good one."

"I'm not joking."

Amane frowned and looked at Yuuta, but Yuuta seemed slightly relieved and laughed like he was poking fun at him, so Amane just snorted and left it at that.

"Amane, welcome."

Amane got home, changed, and headed into the living room where Mahiru, who had gotten home before him, was sitting. She patted her lap with a smile.

Not understanding, he stood there staring at Mahiru, who patted her thighs again, maintaining her gentle smile.

As he was staring at her, still confused, her smile turned strained.

"I got the feeling that you were in a bad mood," she said.

Apparently even Mahiru had seen right through him. Actually, if Yuuta had been able to sniff it out, then it went without saying that Mahiru had, too. He had been hoping he could hide it from her, so his expression sank when he realized that would be impossible. Mahiru just gave him a bemused and knowing smile.

"Because it's you, Amane, I knew that you wouldn't outright refuse to go along with it, but that you probably internally hated the idea. Was I wrong?"

"…You're right, but listen—"

"And so, I thought I'd do something to fix your mood."

"Do you always say it that directly when you're trying to cheer someone up?"

"Heh-heh. Are you mad?"

"…You already know the answer, and you still asked anyway. Where'd you get that habit from?"

"From you, Amane."

When she put it that way, he had no response besides pursing his lips.

Mahiru gave him a little smile and patted her lap again.

Tempted by her inviting thighs beneath a conservative, claret-colored skirt, Amane hesitantly took a seat in a spot a little distance away from Mahiru, then laid down and gently rested his head in her lap.

He turned his face to look up at her and found her smiling down at him. Then he felt her pale, slim fingers slip into his black hair.

"…Amane, are you worrying about me?"

"There's that, too, and…I just don't want to show you off to other guys."

"Out of jealousy?"

"Jealousy or possessiveness, I don't know… I really hated how it felt."

He knew that he was being immature and selfish, so he was a little embarrassed confessing how he felt. He turned his face toward Mahiru's stomach.

When he did, Mahiru let out a sigh and a little laugh, and gently combed through his hair with her fingers, soothing and comforting him.

"Well, it's not like I'm really fond of the idea of wearing that outfit in public, but it's already been decided."

"…Mm."

"I did get them to promise me one thing before I agreed, though."

"What promise?"

"That I get to show my outfit to you first."

Reflexively, he turned his face back and looked up at Mahiru and saw her wearing a bashful smile that just oozed impishness.

"You'll be the first person who gets to see and, um... There will probably be a lot of customers who come to see me, but there's only one person, um, who I'll call...Master."

The second half was halting and hesitant, but she still managed to say it.

Amane's cheeks flared.

He stared straight at her, without averting his gaze, until finally, she apparently couldn't stand it anymore and pushed the cushion beside her into his face. She was gentle, so he was still able to breathe, but he got the message loud and clear that she wanted him to look away.

The haze of emotions that had been swirling deep in Amane's chest were still roiling, but something new...a kind of ticklish feeling, joined the mix.

His heart was overflowing with a feeling that had to be love.

"In that case, I think I'll manage," he said.

"Good," she replied.

Mahiru was still covering his face with the cushion. He couldn't see her, but he could imagine the expression on her face. Amane smiled a little and turned on his side, and buried his face in Mahiru's belly.

Chapter 5

Acceptance Is Key

Ultimately, it was decided that Amane's class would host a café for the culture festival.

When it was announced, all Amane could do was make a face as if he'd swallowed something bitter. He was as dour as the other boys were excited. They were probably eagerly anticipating seeing Mahiru, Chitose, and the other good-looking girls wait on the customers.

Amane knew he couldn't attempt to overturn a decision that had already been made, so he was obediently playing along, but when it came time to take measurements, he was a little defiant.

"No, it won't look good on me, so—"

"We don't know that until you try it on. Come on, give up already, it's a done deal."

"Fujimiyaaa, just surrenderrr!"

"So you're already fully resigned, Kadowaki...?"

"Only because I assumed something like this was going to happen."

According to the person in charge of negotiating for the costumes, they had worked out how to borrow them without issue. Now they wanted to quickly confirm the number of costumes that the class needed, and that meant that it was measuring time for the students who would be waiting on the customers.

…However, Amane had nothing but complaints about the fact that he had been voluntold.

Itsuki had read too much into things, suggesting that he "Use this time with Miss Shiina" and that "Anything could happen," but Amane just wished that he'd been warned ahead of time.

"Huh, Amane…did you get bigger?"

"Hey, that's rude. I haven't gained any weight. I'm actually living a healthier lifestyle."

"Ha-hah, meaning that your little wife is taking good care of you."

"I don't wanna hear it."

Amane felt embarrassed that Itsuki had called Mahiru his wife. Itsuki answered this disgruntled response with his usual teasing laugh.

"Well, I don't think you're fatter. Maybe more muscular?"

"That might be possible. Thanks to Kadowaki's strength training."

"What's that? Tell me more."

Amane told Itsuki to ask Yuuta about it if he wanted to know so badly. Then he glanced over at the other boys who were also being measured. They were talking about something among themselves, but they were being very secretive about it, which made him anxious.

When he strained his ears to catch their conversation, he could just barely hear them talking about Mahiru in excited voices.

"Miss Shiina in a maid costume…awesome!"

"She's getting measured in a different classroom right now. I bet her measurements are incredible."

"Yeah, I mean, they're huge, all right."

"She's way curvier than that Shirakawa girl she's always with."

"If Akazawa hears you, you're a dead man."

"Nah, Itsuki knows that she hasn't got much…he said it was a little more than a handful…"

"Anyway, I'm jealous that Fujimiya can keep Miss Shiina all to himself."

Amane thought of a couple jabs he could have made at the boys, asking if that was how they always looked at other people's girlfriends, or maybe he should mention that Itsuki was liable to be even more angry if he overheard them. He stared at the other boys without even trying to hide his contempt.

"...I wish you guys would at least keep it down a little."

"Ack, you heard us, Fujimiya?"

He wished they wouldn't fantasize about other people's girlfriends like that. But at the same time, he knew that it was immature to get too worked up, so he held it in. Besides, no matter how much they fantasized, the only person who would have the opportunity to lay their eyes on the real thing was Amane, so he could afford to play it cool.

Itsuki also seemed to have noticed them if his scary smile was anything to judge by. Chitose would have been furious if she'd overheard, but he didn't have the slightest inclination to repeat anything he heard, and he suspected everyone would treat it like a confidential discussion.

"I mean, come on... We can't help it."

"Not when it comes to that angel. They're always hidden by her blazer and vest, but they're substantial... Hey, Fujimiya, how are they in real life?"

The vulgar talk had probably come out because there were only boys in the room at the moment.

With expectant eyes turned toward him, Amane shrugged, conscious not to let a wrinkle form in his brow.

"I'm not really sure how to answer that," he replied. "You can see what they're like."

"Don't dodge the question!"

"I really don't know what to say."

"Like, are we talking apples or melons here?"

"And some fruits are firmer than others, you know?"

"You're so annoying!"

"You're the annoying one!"

Why should I have to tell other guys about my girlfriend's measurements? Amane didn't even know her exact size in the first place. Well, actually, he did know her cup size, because when they had stayed at his parents' house, he had accidentally seen some of Mahiru's laundry. But there was obviously no way he was going to say that out loud.

Amane pulled back from his classmates, who were pressing in awfully close. They drew even nearer, their enthusiasm only building. He looked at Itsuki for help, and all he got was a laugh and a shrug. He didn't seem interested in helping.

"Anyway, I don't know."

"Don't lie to us, man."

"I'm not."

"Ah, you guys? I can tell you that what Amane's saying isn't a lie." Itsuki reluctantly offered this meager bit of assistance.

Once Amane and the boys hounding him were all looking at Itsuki, he grinned cheerfully. "After all, even when he's alone with her at home, Amane doesn't lay a finger on Miss Shiina. That's why he'd have no way of knowing."

At Itsuki's words, the classroom fell deathly silent.

"...Fujimiya, you can't be a real man."

"Is that why you didn't show any interest in those gravure magazines?"

"No!" Amane objected. "Itsuki, don't say it in such a weird way—I don't do anything because I respect Mahiru's wishes, that's all!"

"Some would say that makes you a chicken."

"Listen, you—"

"You know, normally…being alone together like that, you only get there if she's already accepted what might happen, right? Girls aren't stupid, so she must know it's a possibility."

"Ah, but these two are the kind of sincere, pure, and innocent couple that's so rare to see these days. It sounds like they think it's too early for that sort of thing. They're naive, all right. Real virgins. In fact, they're a kind of endangered species that we need to protect, so don't say anything uncalled for."

"Hey, Itsuki, whose side are you on?"

"I'm on your side. Always am, pal."

"I find that hard to believe…!"

Thanks to Itsuki's words, the boys gathered around Amane looked at him either with pity or with lukewarm smiles. Amane scowled at their bemused expressions.

"I'm not really that naive," he insisted, "And if I could, of course I'd like to do stuff, but I'm thinking about Mahiru's future and whatever, and holding back, that's all…"

"Uh-huh."

"Hey, don't smirk like that… Hey, what's with you guys, stop looking at me!" Amane snapped at them.

He wanted to be anywhere but here, but the pity and amusement in their faces only grew. Dissatisfied, Amane threw the tape measure at Itsuki, their temporary ringleader.

"…Um, Amane? For some reason, all of the boys are giving me weird looks. Do you know the reason for that?"

"I dunno."

The girls had also finished getting their measurements and had rejoined the class. But Mahiru had sensed that she was getting some strange looks from the boys, and she had snuck over to ask Amane about it.

Amane himself was getting some awkward looks from the girls, so he wanted to ask Mahiru the same question.

"I'm getting some weird looks from the girls myself...Mahiru, did you say something?"

"N-nothing that would harm your reputation."

"Meaning you *did* say something that wouldn't harm my reputation?"

"J-just what I usually talk about with you, and how we spend our time together. Don't worry."

"What did you say, exactly?"

"...I told them that you're gentlemanly and nice."

"Not you, too!"

"Not me, too, what?"

"No, never mind."

There was no way that he could tell Mahiru that the boys had been teasing him for having no guts, so although he was raging inside, he answered her in a calm voice, and ruffled Mahiru's hair as she stared at him in puzzlement.

"...Could you try to avoid sharing too much with people? It's embarrassing for me."

"S-sure, okay. For me, it's...it's helpful for me, though, because I learn all sorts of things from everybody else."

"I just can't help but worry about what they might be putting in your head."

Although Chitose had also been planting quite a few unnecessary ideas in Mahiru's mind, Amane was afraid that the other girls were also teaching her weird stuff. He was sure that even Chitose restrained herself to a certain degree, but if he could, he would have liked to check what she was putting into Mahiru's mind.

"…I don't really think it's going to cause any problems for you though, Amane."

"I'm getting some serious looks from the girls, literally as we speak."

"W-well…there's nothing we can do about that."

"I feel like there could be."

"Hey, you two, you can flirt if you want, but I'd like to get back to the agenda before too long, so quit making a show of it."

Itsuki, their executive committee member, was standing in front of the lectern looking around the classroom and shrugged.

Amane and Mahiru weren't trying to flirt, but with the way things were going, it was pointless to argue.

"Well, leaving those two aside, let's decide on the food and drink menu for our café. We really should have decided this first, but there was the more immediate issue of securing costumes. Ah, Kido, will you pass on our sizes to your contact and count up how many of each costume we need? The boys' measurements are here. Resist the urge to use this information for evil."

It was easy to tell how good Itsuki was at managing people when he briskly rattled off instructions along with the boys' measurements to the student who was in charge of the costumes.

"Okay, first, we can't serve anything raw. There are limits to the days and times we can reserve the cooking room. After considering safety and how long things will keep, we're more or less limited to baked goods and drinks. Any objections?"

"Nope!"

"Chi, you're not going to make any strange additions, okay?"

"How rude!"

Chitose had committed a prior offense on Valentine's Day, but that had ultimately only involved her friends, so they could expect that she wouldn't do anything similar this time around.

"Okay, so that brings us to the drinks. We're a café, so I think coffee, tea, and juice will do it. If you have any other suggestions for food or drinks, let's hear 'em. I could only come up with obvious stuff."

"Ooh, me! How about ice cream? I want to make cream sodas!"

"I think it's a good idea, but how would we keep it cold? It's possible if we work on the assumption that we'll be prepping everything in the kitchen and carrying them over, but it'll use up a lot of the freezers, so I'll have to check with the student council. For now, I'll keep it on here as a possibility."

"What about light meals?"

"I did take that into consideration, but given how much work and time we'd need to commit to cooking, it's probably not the best idea. There's a big difference between serving premade treats and making stuff to order. Plus, the only things we could cook properly would be things like hot dogs and hot sandwiches. Another class is already planning on making hot dogs, and I'm pretty sure they'd be upset if we stole their customers."

"Scratch that, then."

Itsuki smoothly moved the conversation along and made notes about everything they discussed. Amane marveled at how he conducted the meeting, and Mahiru seemed to feel the same way.

"We're in good hands," she said with a quiet chuckle.

"All right, then. That about does it for our list. I'll put it all together and submit it to the student council and get them to check it over. As for securing our drinks... For the coffee, I know someone who has a business selling coffee beans wholesale, so I'll go talk to him. Maybe he'd be willing to give us a discount in exchange for some promotion. We're going to all this trouble, so I hope folks will be impressed by our flavors, too."

"Whoo! That's our guy!"

"Don't fall in love. All you'll get is a no-thank-you from me."

It was one of Itsuki's great skills to get things done while cracking flippant jokes the whole time.

Marveling at his friend's impossible cheerfulness and command of the room, Amane considered the upcoming exhibit their class was hashing out bit by bit, and he quietly let out a sigh.

Last year I got by with just decorating a haunted house...

On the one hand, he was annoyed that, for some reason, he was getting stuck serving customers this year. On the other hand, he also felt deeply emotional about the idea of participating in such a typical student event.

The Amane of yesteryear had thought that all the time and effort that went into the culture festival was a waste, but...now he had Mahiru by his side. It wouldn't be so bad for the two of them to make some memories.

"Is something the matter?" Mahiru asked.

"No, I was just thinking I better work hard at the culture festival."

"Heh-heh, that's right. I'm looking forward to seeing you serving customers, Amane."

"I'm not very good at being friendly."

He answered her teasing rather bluntly, but Mahiru just smiled.

Chapter 6

Who Does That Smile Work On?

Under Itsuki's direction, preparations for the culture festival proceeded swiftly. Part of that was because it was everyone's second culture festival, and they were steady hands at this. However, the boys and girls in the class also clearly had ulterior motives, which played a large part in their eagerness.

They were doing everything they could to get ready, on top of their daily classwork, so things were quite busy. However, in an unusual turn for Amane, he found himself enjoying the work so much that he didn't find it tiresome.

"Hey, there's a mistake on these flyers! We haven't put them up yet, so go fix them. We definitely can't use them if the school's address is wrong!"

"Do you know what happened to the tablecloths? I heard that someone went and bought some, but I can't find them anywhere!"

"With our pricing, even if we don't sell much, we can expect to bring in about this much, so…"

As they listened to the hustle and bustle of their classmates going about their duties, Amane and the other students who were going to serve the customers were being coached by the team leader in charge of customer service.

"Fujimiya, uh…smile."

"…Smile."

"That's a grimace!"

Ayaka Kido, the girl in their class who worked part-time at a café and was in charge of procuring the costumes, was also coaching their servers. Her smile was starting to slip as she critiqued Amane's stiff, unconvincing attempt at a grin.

He had spoken with her several times before the summer break, but he hadn't really interacted with her since then. Now that they were stuck together, he wasn't entirely sure how to act around her. Undaunted even by the unsociable Amane, Kido was doing her best to teach him the fundamentals of customer service, but it was all very strange to him and he just wasn't getting it.

Amane wasn't incapable of smiling, but according to Kido, he definitely looked awkward.

"Hmm. A normal smile would do just fine, you know. The more you think about it, the weirder it gets. You look so stiff. Relax more, relax."

"You say that, but, like, it just happens whenever I think about serving customers."

"Imagine your customers are sweet potatoes. That should help."

"Potatoes?"

"Eggs might work better for Amane," Mahiru added with a giggle. She was receiving the same orientation.

After taking care of him for nearly a year, Mahiru knew that Amane loved eggs. But it wasn't like he randomly smiled at raw eggs, so ultimately, her suggestion wasn't the most helpful.

That's not really the problem, Amane thought.

But Mahiru seemed to be enjoying herself, so he didn't offer any kind of retort and just scratched his cheek.

"Well, lots of people would say that being natural is better than forcing it," Itsuki suggested. "So just do whatever'll help you relax, Amane."

"Exactly who would say that my natural attitude is any better?"

"The girls in our class? At least that seemed to be the consensus when I peeked in on them while they were with Miss Shiina."

"I guess I just don't like being looked at."

"You're not showing off for anyone?"

"As if."

Amane glared at Itsuki. He was sure that Itsuki was riling him up on purpose.

But all he got in response was an exasperated, "This guy's really dense…"

For the time being, he responded simply. "Shut up."

Mahiru was smiling quietly, and her cheeks were slightly flushed. Her eyes kept running over Amane and she blushed even more than before. She seemed like she might be feeling a bit self-conscious.

Starting with Ayaka, all the other girls nodded in agreement.

"You're at your most charming when you're spending time with Miss Shiina, Fujimiya," Ayaka said.

"What about me is charming…?"

"It's like…some sort of aura you give off."

"Aura…"

"You catch me by surprise sometimes, you know?"

He didn't understand what Ayaka meant, but Mahiru seemed to have some idea. She was trying to hide her embarrassment. But he could see that in her eyes, mixed in with that embarrassment, there was a hint of anxiety.

Ayaka seemed to notice as well, because she broke into a big smile and waved both hands in a gesture of denial.

"It's okay, it's okay. I've got a boyfriend. I'm not interested in stealing someone else's."

"I—I wasn't worried about that..."

"You don't have to hide it! I know what it feels like when someone starts paying attention to your boyfriend. But I'm only interested in guys with big muscles. Fujimiya's too skinny, so he's definitely not my type!"

"I feel like she just called me a bean sprout."

Amane had thought he had been putting on a decent amount of muscle. It was fairly disappointing to hear that he was still too skinny. Itsuki had even complimented him, telling him that he had gotten stronger, but apparently Itsuki's standards were fairly low.

"A-Amane isn't a bean sprout," Mahiru interjected. "Sure, he has a light complexion, but...well...w-when he takes off his shirt, he's actually...pretty muscular."

"Oh, he looks good with his shirt off?"

"You're gonna give people the wrong idea! Don't say weird things like that, Mahiru."

"...But you're quite well-built."

"Never mind that. You're going to be the one who feels embarrassed about this later, Mahiru."

He wanted her to realize that she was admitting, in her own words, that she'd had the opportunity to see and touch his bare skin.

The reality was that they had been wearing bathing suits, so it wasn't like he had anything to feel guilty about. But to anyone listening, it wouldn't have been difficult to interpret her words to mean that they had already been intimate together. However, Mahiru had also let word get out that Amane was a total gentleman, so it also seemed like people might assume that they hadn't done anything.

Amane was relieved when Mahiru declined to say anything further on the subject. Just as he'd expected, the other students around them were giving the couple tepid looks. Without thinking about it, he clicked his tongue. Mostly at Itsuki.

"Huh? Why are you looking at me like that?"

"Because your grinning is pissing me off."

"Whoa, don't make this about me," Itsuki insisted. "Come on, no more love talk. Time to practice," he said, urging Amane to set his personal matters aside,

Amane clicked his tongue at Itsuki again before turning back to Ayaka with discontent still written all over his face. Ayaka just laughed.

"Well, I can see that you two are passionate, and that's enough for me. As long as you welcome the customers with a half-decent smile, Fujimiya, it'll be fine. The way you naturally carry yourself is already nice, so if you can greet people in the way I taught you, I don't think we'll have any problems."

"I've never thought that I carry myself well."

Amane didn't think that he was clumsy, but he didn't think that he was especially graceful either, so he was puzzled to hear her say that.

But Mahiru smiled knowingly. "I think it's probably because you watched your parents growing up," she said. "The two of them are so graceful."

"I don't know if I agree, especially when it comes to my mom, but yeah, I guess she's not clumsy."

"Does that mean that you're close with Fujimiya's family, too, Miss Shiina?"

"K-Kido..."

"Sorry, sorry!"

Amane turned a sour look on the giggling Ayaka, but that just made her laugh even harder. She and Mahiru together were both looking at him in amusement.

With two weeks until the school festival, the class got word that the costumes they had requested had arrived.

"Okay, these are the outfits that came in! I'll hand them out, so just wait a second, okay! I'll let you know when it's time to try them on, so wait for that too, please."

With a smile, Ayaka handed each of them a costume. When she came to Amane's desk, she handed his outfit over with a big grin. "Right, here you go. Oh, Fujimiya, later on, you can go to the classroom we've reserved as a dressing room by yourself, okay?"

"Why by myself?"

"Mmm. Special case."

"What does that mean?"

"A little request, from Miss Shiina. One that I'm inclined to grant. She said she wanted to show it to you first, so…"

Ayaka mentioned in passing that he didn't need to worry because of course she had already gotten permission from all the other girls, and while Amane felt a little guilty about it, he was delighted that Mahiru had gone so far as to make the request.

Feeling grateful, especially to Ayaka, who had willingly accepted that request, as well as to the other girls in their class, Amane smiled and said, "Thank you."

And so, at the allotted time, Amane waited outside the door of the classroom where he had been told that Mahiru was getting changed.

It went without saying, but the curtains had been pulled closed. Originally, they had planned for the boys and girls to get changed in their respective locker rooms and then practice waiting tables in costume. Instead, they borrowed a classroom because walking through the school in maid outfits with long swishy skirts would cause a stir, and with the hallways overflowing with props and paint, there was a distinct possibility of tearing the costumes or getting them dirty.

What is this—I'm nervous?

When Amane thought about the fact that there was a girl changing clothes just on the other side of the door, he felt kind of awkward and nervous. She was his girlfriend, and he had seen her undressed before—nearly in her underwear—but putting that aside, he still couldn't calm down.

As he was leaning his back against the door, waiting in silence, he heard a somewhat stiff voice say from within the classroom, "You can come in now."

Mahiru being Mahiru, she was probably just as nervous. He smiled a little and followed her prompting to enter the classroom.

He closed the door behind him, and looked at Mahiru, who was standing a short distance from the door.

Mahiru was wearing a waitress uniform with long sleeves and a long skirt that went down to her ankles.

It was a classic type of maid outfit with some modern updates. The outfit was a set, consisting of a long, navy blue dress, with long sleeves that puffed up at the upper arm and almost looked like they were inflated with air, as well as an apron to go on top.

Kido had said that when they wore uniforms with miniskirts at her job, they put on petticoat to make them puff out. But the dress Mahiru was wearing had a long skirt, so it was designed to be narrow and form a smooth silhouette.

Frills went all around the apron, but the outfit exposed almost no skin, producing a tidy, clean impression. Under the hem of the long skirt, he could see Mahiru's ankles, covered by black tights.

The black tights actually belonged to Mahiru. She wore them year-round, so that she wouldn't carelessly show any skin at school, and she was wearing them now, too.

"How does it look?"

Mahiru gently tilted her head, and her side bangs that she had left untied swayed gently.

Since her role was to serve customers and carry food, her long, flaxen hair had been gathered into a bun on the back of her head and secured under a chignon cap so that it wouldn't get in the way.

"...It looks even better on you than I imagined."

"Does it? I'm glad. It's my first time wearing a costume like this, so..."

He offered her his honest praise and got a bashful smile in return.

It was certainly true that the outfit looked good on Mahiru, because she was so beautiful. But more than anything, Amane was surprised by how well the costume fit Mahiru's personality.

By nature, Mahiru had a helpful disposition, so that probably made the outfit suit her even better.

Looking at her smiling softly, Amane couldn't help but feel like he didn't want to let her serve anyone else.

"Amane?"

"Huh? ...Ah, sorry. It looks so great on you, I don't want to show anyone else and lose it."

"Heh-heh, lose what?"

"My...enthusiasm?"

"Well, I promise I'll play with your hair later, so please bear with it. After all, I also don't love the idea of letting other people see you in your butler's outfit..."

"Mine won't be anything special, so it's okay."

"It's not okay at all!"

©Hanekoto

Mahiru had gotten worked up for some reason, so Amane apologized meekly, "Sorry."

"No, I'm sorry." Mahiru also seemed to think she had been a tad forceful.

"...Amane, ever since you had your makeover, you've gotten more approachable and, um, I've even heard other girls saying how good you look."

"Well, as the person in question, I don't remember hearing a thing."

"It's not the sort of thing you would say to the person you're talking about. They only talk about it with other girls...and I'm here, so they're not going to openly approach you, you know?"

It sent a little chill down his spine when he wondered what the girls were saying about him in private. But from what Mahiru said, it sounded like opinions of him were largely favorable. However, he doubted anyone was actually into him. At best, he had been getting lukewarm looks.

And it was hard to imagine that any girl would approach him, since he was already dating someone. Actually, he firmly refused to believe it was possible.

From Amane's point of view, there wasn't a single girl in school who felt that way, so Mahiru's words didn't really ring true to him.

The fact that Amane only half believed what Mahiru said must have shown on his face.

Mahiru stuck out her lip in an adorable pout.

"Listen, when it's just the girls, we talk *really* openly. Like, how is this boy in his relationship with girls, how's his personality, how's his experience. Honestly, we talk about things that we would *never* let boys hear us say."

"Just what has my girlfriend gotten dragged into?"

"That's what girl talk is like. Almost nothing is off-limits, and everyone says exactly what's on their minds... And in those honest conversations, I've heard them say that you're a cool guy, and I guess I can't help but get anxious. It sets me on edge."

Mahiru squirmed like she was finding this all very difficult to say. She was a perfectly charming maid, and Amane felt a surge of something like guilt, with just a touch of sadistic satisfaction.

"By the way, what kind of things are they saying?"

"Um, that you seem nice, and gentlemanly…and that it seems like, if you like a girl, she's the only one you look at, and how great that is and stuff."

"Well, they're probably right. I only have eyes for you, Mahiru."

It seemed only natural to Amane that he would only be interested in his partner. It would just be rude to go chasing after another girl when he was in a relationship already.

He wasn't dating Mahiru with such shallow commitment. Amane had often been told that members of the Fujimiya family were deeply affectionate and devoted, and Amane truly had no intention of looking at anyone besides Mahiru.

"I mean, you're the same way, right Mahiru? You're not out there checking out other guys?"

"I would never!"

"Then you don't have to worry… You're the only one for me, Mahiru, the only one I'm looking at. But still, I hate the idea of anyone looking at you funny, so I guess I didn't want to let anyone see you looking like that."

At that point, Amane went back to the original topic. In response, Mahiru frowned just a little, then pushed her forehead against his upper arm several times in a kind of head-butt.

"…We'll both have to hang in there, then."

"Yeah."

"That said, I wanted to keep you all to myself. That's what I was saying."

"Me too."

Amane gently patted Mahiru's back as she ground her forehead into his arm, and she raised her head and stared directly at him.

"...I want to see your butler's uniform soon, too, Amane."

"The boys are borrowing the room next. We'll make our debut soon, so be patient."

Amane was getting to see Mahiru first as a special favor from Itsuki and Chitose, and Ayaka as well, but rightfully, they were meant to debut their costumes all at once.

Before long, it would be time for the boys to put on their borrowed clothes as well.

"...It's not going to be anything special, you know?"

"Don't say that. I'm looking forward to it."

She turned a smile on him that showed it was not flattery, that she really felt that way. Feeling unspeakably uneasy, all Amane could do was scratch his cheek and answer, "Wait for me, but don't expect too much."

"How was Miss Shiina?"

"How was she...? It looked good on her."

It was time for the male waiters to change clothes, but the other boys seemed more interested in hearing from Amane, who had been the first to see Mahiru in her maid costume.

All Amane could think to say was that the costume looked good on her. His classmates were obviously disappointed by his simple reaction, and looked at him with exasperated faces.

"Come on, there's got to be more. Give us your reaction."

"I don't know what else to say... It's not like there was any chance it wasn't going to look good."

"Well, I guess that's true. It is Miss Shiina, after all."

"I want her to serve me."

"I want her to call me Master with a smile on her face…"

"She's obviously not going to be waiting on your tables or serving you guys."

"That's just selfish…so selfish…you could at least let us dream."

"I'm doing you a favor by crushing your dreams that will never come true."

"Savage!"

Amane talked freely with his cackling classmates while they were preparing, cracking lighthearted jokes (though some of them did truly seem upset). He occasionally got a slap on the back along with confessions of jealousy as they went back and forth.

Fundamentally, Amane's circle of friends was quite small, and he wasn't especially motivated to form new connections. But all of his classmates were good-natured kids, and he didn't mind making friends with them while working on a project together.

As he went along with the banter, deliberately shooting back curt responses to the boys' jokes, he pulled on the clothes that had been laid out for him.

The outfits for the boys were simple: a set of slacks and a navy blue jacket that was so dark it almost looked black, plus a gray waistcoat. The suits were cut in a slim fit that matched each person's physique, which instantly created a sense of elegance. With the addition of white gloves, everyone really looked the part. It was an incredible transformation.

Of course, since the costumes were all borrowed from the same place, the boys' uniforms had matched the girls' maid outfits well, and when they lined up together, they were sure to look like the real deal.

When he'd first seen the outfits, Amane had thought they looked stiff and hard to move in, but now that he was actually wearing one, the fabric had more give to it than he had expected.

"Whoa, Itsuki looks like a total playboy butler. The cheeky kind you see in manga all the time."

"Huh, why are you talking about me?"

It sounded like Itsuki had also finished getting changed, and the other boys were teasing him.

When Amane glanced over, he saw that the other boys' assessment was true, and that to put it nicely, Itsuki made a very cheerful-looking butler. To put it not so nicely, he gave off a vaguely insincere air.

"Mm, you look kinda tacky."

"You too, Amane? No fair! All while you…damn, you're sporting some serious style to show off to Miss Shiina."

"Of course. Why even mention it?"

Since Amane was going to show his outfit to Mahiru, he was styling himself perfectly. He had even slicked part of his hair back to make himself look sharper than usual.

He wasn't planning to go for the fully swept-back look he often saw in advertisements, but even Amane could pull off this basic look.

"He's serious…this guy's serious…"

"Amane, you were so unenthusiastic about this before, but you're really getting into it."

"For some reason, my girlfriend is expecting something from me, so I've gotta take it seriously," Amane answered.

"There he goes…talking about his girlfriend again…"

"I mean, if you guys had girlfriends expecting something from you, you'd try hard too, I bet."

"Knock it off, Fujimiya. You're making us single guys depressed."

"Ah…sorry…"

"Don't apologize, you'll just make us more miserable…"

Amane decided, just this once, to obediently accept the casual ribbing from his classmates. He shrugged at Itsuki, who was still smiling, but also looking a little down at being called tacky.

"Well, seeing Itsuki should make Chitose happy."

"You got that right. But you can bet she'll laugh at me and just say 'Itsuki the playboy!'"

"Definitely."

Amane chuckled quietly. It seemed like the sort of thing Chitose would say, without even trying to tease him.

Itsuki jabbed him in the ribs, so in response, Amane slapped Itsuki on the back to cheer him up. "Anyway, Kadowaki's gonna get all the attention, don't you think?"

"Nah, the girls told me there was demand for 'princely types, and funny types, and cool types, and baby faces, too.'"

"Kokonoe's got to be the baby face, too bad. And the funny type, that's definitely you."

Among the boys who had been recruited to be waiters because they were good-looking, Makoto had the smallest build, and arguably a very unique look. Girls regularly called him cute, and he never seemed too happy about it, but this time he seemed even more irate than usual.

Amane looked Makoto up and down as he dressed himself impeccably, wearing a scowl of discontent. For better or worse, he was dainty and had a boyish face, so it seemed like he would fulfill a particular demand.

Kazuya, Makoto's good friend, was going to be working behind the scenes. The reason was that Kazuya was fairly careless, and his build was sturdier than the other boys, so he had been deemed more suited for manual labor than serving customers.

"…Kazuya, you traitor…damn you…"

Everyone heard the curses streaming from Makoto's adorable face, but pretended like they didn't.

"Oh wow, Itsuki, you look great! Like a real playboy!"

In the classroom, it was time for all the servers to get together and reveal their costumes. As expected, Chitose called Itsuki a playboy with a grin on her face.

Itsuki knew that he could come off as a flirt, and he didn't deny it, but he did get a somewhat distant look in his eyes. "That bad, huh...?"

Given the way his friend usually talked and acted, Amane didn't argue, either.

Chitose was also going to be one of the waitstaff, so she was dressed in a maid outfit as well.

There must have been two different patterns because the outfit she had on wasn't cut to the same modest design as Mahiru's. Instead, it was a cute and heavily decorated number with a skirt that ended several centimeters above the knee.

There were frills poking out below the hem, and Chitose's long, slender legs were covered by white knee socks. The combination of the short skirt and the frilly apron really made her look like the embodiment of the modern idea of a maid.

"Anyway, how is it? Does it look good on me?"

"Of course it does. You look good in anything, Chi."

"Says the one who was rolling on the floor laughing before, when I borrowed Mahiru's clothes and put them on to show you."

"Aw, but that was 'cause of the size thing."

"Itsuki..."

"Sorry."

Even the (so-called) playboy Itsuki became meek when his girlfriend chided him. It was Itsuki's own fault for provoking her, so Amane didn't get involved. Also, because he could see that if he intervened, the repercussions would spill over to him.

Amane could see that aside from Chitose, all the other girls who would be serving customers were wearing their maid outfits, too, and even though it was his own class's exhibition, he marveled that they had managed to put together something so impressive. A café where customers were greeted by such striking staff was sure to get people talking.

Ayaka, who had orchestrated the costume reveal, was wearing the same type of maid costume as Mahiru. She walked over to Amane, grinning.

"Ah, Fujimiya, you're dressed up perfectly, too, huh? That's the spirit!"

"Mahiru's expecting something from me, so..."

"Heh-heh, what a good boyfriend you are. Look, Miss Shiina, it's your boyfriend as a butler!"

Ayaka beckoned Mahiru over with a cheery smile, but for some reason, she didn't come any closer. Amane wondered whether she didn't like his outfit, but her face was red, and she was squirming, so that didn't seem to be the problem.

When she saw how Mahiru was acting, Ayaka gave Amane with a broad grin. "She was fidgeting with anticipation the whole time, and I think she probably got more than she was picturing."

Then she turned back to Mahiru. "Come on Miss Shiina, it's a wasted opportunity if you don't see your boy close-up, ya know? Besides, you're working your shift as a pair, so you'd better get used to it now!"

Through the scheming of their classmates that had been spearheaded by Itsuki, Amane and Mahiru would be working at the same time. This was partly out of concern to protect her from any sort of sexual harassment, but also out of consideration, so that after the shift change, the two of them could walk around together.

Ayaka pushed Mahiru on the back, and Mahiru approached him hesitantly.

"It doesn't suit me?" Amane asked.

"Wh-who said that?! You look really wonderful, like it's not even you…"

"That different, huh? What are you seeing?"

"…You look, well, sexier than usual."

"But I'm actually wearing more clothes than normal. My outfits are more casual at home, right?"

"Sometimes dressing up is better!"

Amane was perplexed when Mahiru insisted very strongly on this point. But for some reason, the other girls were also giving him knowing nods, so it didn't seem like he could really argue with what she had said.

Mahiru was still looking up at him with flushed cheeks, fidgeting. She was liable to drive the other boys crazy with her cuteness, so he knew he had to stop her before too long.

"…Mahiru, please don't look at anyone else like that. You'll kill them."

"Same to you, Amane."

"Yeah, yeah."

"S-so careless…"

She seemed dissatisfied. But when it came to their looks, Mahiru and Amane were on completely different levels, so it was virtually impossible that he would captivate boys and girls alike like she would.

So he brushed her comment off, signaling that it was something they didn't need to worry about. But Mahiru still didn't seem convinced and shook Amane a little by the upper arm.

"Welcome!"

"Whoa…"

As soon as the costume unveiling was done, it was time to practice waiting on customers. But they didn't get much practicing done.

©Hanekoto

Their eyes were blinded by a dazzling light. The boys were knocked out thanks to Mahiru's professional smile.

Their classmates who volunteered to play the customers all went to bits when they saw her smile. An angel's smile was a great and terrible thing.

Even the boy who'd braved the first attack was succumbing with a smile as he was shown to his table. Amane could feel his cheek begin twitching, all the while thinking that they would be in trouble if he couldn't get her to tone it down a bit.

"The angel is too powerful…tell Miss Shiina to stop, Amane."

"That smile isn't even at full power yet."

"What?! She's got more…?!

"This is no time to be amused. It's no laughing matter, at all."

As he watched from the sidelines, Amane thought that Mahiru's smile still looked very artificial.

It was what he would consider a polite, professional smile. An elegant smile, just for the purpose of serving customers. He had a feeling that if Mahiru put more heart into her smile, the boys would be completely helpless.

Even some of the girls were gazing at Mahiru in fascination, so the power of the Angel Smile was obvious.

"…We're not getting much practice in, huh?"

Ayaka, who had been watching this all go down, was of course grimacing.

Amane was used to spending time with Mahiru, and maybe that's why he had underestimated her destructive power. But by her very nature, Mahiru had an incredible beauty and presence that just enthralled people. He should have expected something like this would happen.

"I don't think she'll have any trouble actually serving customers, but…it will be a problem if she makes all the customers dizzy, won't it?"

"Sorry."

"No, none of this is your fault, or hers…," Ayaka said, with a distant look in her eyes.

Amane felt really terrible for Ayaka, but even he was helpless to stop it.

"…I guess we'd probably better stock a lot of cold drinks."

"Yeah…let's serve them ice-cold."

Mahiru's effect seemed to be blanketing the classroom in a terrible heat, so the two of them decided in the course of their conversation that they would also get someone to monitor the air conditioning.

"But still, if we don't make her go easy, that's gonna be an issue."

"You're right, there'll be casualties."

"I mean, there might be casualties anyway, but…this isn't very enjoyable for me at all."

He let his true thoughts show, and Ayaka turned a puzzled look toward him.

"Even if it is for work, my girlfriend is showing all these boys her beautiful smile and I don't love watching it," Amane explained. "You might say I'm being petty, but that's how it is."

He accepted the situation, in theory.

Mahiru was just fulfilling her assigned duties, and the smile Mahiru was wearing was the one she showed to most people, the smile she wore for the outside world. It was not the cherubic, innocent expression that was only for Amane, nor was it her subtly sensual impish smile.

Even so, he felt some discomfort deep in his chest, which he knew was the feeling of jealousy.

Amane shrugged, thinking self-deprecatingly to himself how pathetic that was, and Ayaka looked at him with fresh eyes, not hiding anything.

"So that's how it is? You're completely infatuated with Miss Shiina, eh, Fujimiya?"

"...Would you mind not being quite so direct about it?"

"Eh-heh-heh. I can tell just by looking at her that Miss Shiina is head over heels for you, and here you are, just as madly in love ...I always pegged you for the type who didn't get too attached, Fujimiya, but I guess things are different when it comes to Miss Shiina."

"Please try to put yourself in my shoes. Think about how I feel hearing that from someone else."

"Come on, I can tell just by looking at you that she's super import-ant to you, and that you must really love her. Fujimiya, you usually have a blank look on your face, and you seem a little scary, but when you're with Miss Shiina, your face relaxes and you put on a dopey, happy smile, so it's super clear that she must be special."

Ayaka said this earnestly, without a teasing tone in her voice, so he couldn't just brush it aside. Amane's eyes darted around the room, and Ayaka looked at him with a smile of genuine enjoyment.

"Well, that being the case, I can see that you're burning with jeal-ousy, and I can tell that you're a guy and that you must love Miss Shi-ina, which is heartwarming, I guess, or a nice thing to see, anyway... I'm not crushing on you, though, so don't worry about that, okay?"

"Why would you even say that, then?"

"Oh, because I'm getting that look from Miss Shiina. She's look-ing this way," Ayaka said in a carefree voice, making him realize that Mahiru was looking at him.

The look he was getting from her wasn't necessarily one of suspi-cion, she just looked slightly disapproving. He wasn't being suspected of cheating or anything.

Just as Amane was harboring complicated feelings about Mahiru smiling for the crowd, Mahiru must have been a tiny bit unamused seeing Amane getting along well with another girl.

On the other hand, Mahiru seemed to like Ayaka as a person, so the look in her eyes seemed complicated.

Itsuki had apparently been listening to their conversation. "You get plenty of loving yourself, Amane," he teased.

Ayaka also flattered Amane with a happy smile. "So Fujimiya's well-loved, too, huh?"

Amane frowned for a moment, but looked at Mahiru with a gentle smile of his own.

And so, once the girls' customer service practice was more or less finished, it was the boys' turn.

"I want to try being Kadowaki's customer."

"Ah, no fair, me too!"

"Hang on, you can't just decide for yourself! If you can say that, then the same goes for me!"

"Since when can we nominate ourselves?"

The girls were scrambling to be Yuuta's practice partner. Amane was watching them with a distant look in his eyes, marveling at how incredible girls could be. The fact that Yuuta was single at the moment must have been one reason for their frantic yells.

Amane, who interacted with Yuuta as a friend, knew that Yuuta was a good, honest young man, and that he was attractive both as a friend and as a boy. But even so, seeing how popular he was, Amane was simultaneously impressed and felt a little bit of pity. As he watched from the sidelines, he wondered whether Yuuta had ever had a moment when he could feel at ease.

Yuuta himself was smiling, even though he had a troubled, exhausted look in his eyes.

"Amazing, huh?"

Ayaka was looking on in a carefree manner, staying out of the fray. She made it sound like it was really not her problem and that she was simply an observer in all this. Rather than being amused by it, like Amane, she was gazing at Yuuta with eyes full of pity.

"Kido…you said you had a boyfriend, didn't you?"

Amane recalled her telling him the last time they'd spoken that she had a boyfriend, so that she wouldn't give Mahiru the wrong idea. He understood why she didn't show any interest in Yuuta.

"Yep, I do. He's in another class, though. We were childhood friends. He's got great muscles."

"That's quite an introduction."

"Well, he is my ideal after all. I think he's wonderful, so I've got to compliment him… Ah, of course his muscles aren't the only thing I like about him, you know? He's kind of awkward, but he's a sweet and gentle person."

With a grin, she promised to introduce them if she and Amane ever saw him while they were together, and Amane agreed.

For the time being, the image he had formed of Ayaka's boyfriend was someone hyper macho, but Ayaka was completely unaware of that. With a smile on her face, she set out to calm the small riot that was breaking out over who would be Yuuta's customer, and forcefully clapped her hands together to get everyone's attention.

"Okay ladies, you can take turns being Kadowaki's practice partner. I'll make you a roster, so talk among yourselves and decide on an order. After all, we're gonna practice a bunch of times, so he can make the rounds. That's fair, right? While we're at it, Akazawa, try to take this seriously, okay? This is your opportunity to show off how manly you are."

"Nah, this isn't the kind of job where manliness makes a difference. Yuuta makes it work, though."

"You can't leave everything up to Kadowaki! And don't you just sit back and enjoy the show, Chitose!"

"Huh, but—"

"No buts! For now, stand off to the side with the girls who want to be practice customers while they decide what order to go in, then come report to me. Look, the other boys are available, so everyone get to practicing!"

Amane smiled wryly at Ayaka, who was much more dependable at times like these than Itsuki, who was the one actually supposed to be directing things.

Mahiru approached Amane slowly and stood quietly beside him.

"I'll be your first customer, okay, Amane?"

"I figured as much. But I have to ask, why is everyone making requests?"

"Maybe because all of you turned out so handsomely?"

"Well, I gotta admit, Kadowaki and the others do make fine-looking butlers. He's ideal for the role."

Yuuta, who was smiling like he was at a loss for what to do as he was being swarmed by girls with twinkling eyes, certainly wore his butler's uniform well.

He was a beautiful young man, classically handsome, but gentle and kind, with a cheerful and lively presence; princely, though Yuuta himself plainly disliked that reputation. These kinds of clothes suited him extremely well. Although it really seemed like there weren't many things that wouldn't have suited him.

It wasn't Yuuta's intention at all, but he looked so cool that it was bound to have that effect on the girls. Watching it all go down, Amane felt a little embarrassed about how they would compare when they stood next to each other.

"It certainly does suit Mister Kadowaki well, but...if we're talking about tastes, mine don't run that way."

"If we're talking about tastes, I'll be in trouble if yours don't run my way... You're sure you're happy with me?"

"Of course."

Embarrassment welled up inside him when she answered so decisively, but Mahiru continued with a natural expression, "You're my number one, Amane."

He wasn't about to argue.

...I guess there's my proof that I'm loved.

He was embarrassed, but on the other hand happy, so it was probably inevitable that his lips curled up just a little.

When he covered his mouth with his gloved hand to hide his embarrassment, Mahiru put on a graceful smile that seemed to say she had seen through everything he was thinking.

After that, once the dispute over the slots as Yuuta's practice partner had been settled, Amane and the other boys practiced waiting on customers. It went without saying that Mahiru was Amane's practice partner.

"Welcome. Allow me to show you to your seat."

He tried his best to give Mahiru a natural-looking smile as she entered the classroom in her role as a customer, but for some reason, she froze.

Rather than the smile that he always showed Mahiru at home, he was using a smile for customers she had never seen before, but for some reason it sent Mahiru's gaze darting around frantically.

"Miss, is anything the matter?"

"N-no, nothing at all."

She shook her head vigorously, so her long hair swung back and forth like a whip. Since they were stubbornly maintaining an appropriate distance between staff member and customer, her hair didn't hit him, but if they had been standing at their usual distance, it probably would have.

Feeling relieved that he had the composure to even think about such a thing, Amane guided Mahiru to her table. Since they would be counting the number of patrons at the reception desk by the door, they would be certain that no customer entered the café without a seat available.

"Please take a seat here, and I'll be right with you."

Amane pulled out her chair and smiled at her, and Mahiru sat down, trembling as she did so.

It was probably out of shyness and nervousness, but Amane, who was giving his girlfriend the customer service smile that Ayaka had trained him to use, was the one who was really embarrassed. He didn't know why Mahiru might be feeling embarrassed, but if he had to say, he was even more embarrassed.

For the time being, they were trying to practice, so he purposely ignored Mahiru's reactions as he told her the recommended menu items, wrote down her order, and headed over to the classroom kitch- enette, which they had partitioned off behind a curtain.

"…How do I put it? That was like an ambush."

"I don't understand what you mean."

Even after taking her order, Amane continued to practice his cus- tomer service, looking after her until she left the café when he was finally finished.

He finished his practice with Mahiru as his partner, and when he went over to Ayaka, who was directing things, she nodded at him seri- ously. Mahiru, incidentally, had never managed to regain her calm, from beginning to end, so he was worried that he had made some sort of careless blunder.

"Ah, there was no problem with your service or the way you car- ried yourself."

"But did you see what happened with Mahiru?"

"Wasn't that because you were so cool, Fujimiya? You really looked the part. Hey, do you wanna work part-time at my café? The manager would love you!"

"I'll think about it if I'm ever personally in need of money."

When he implied that he wasn't planning on taking her up on the job at the moment, Ayaka gave him a disappointed smile, then glanced over at Mahiru, who was being fanned with a file folder by Chitose.

"Looks like the culture festival is gonna be rough on Miss Shiina, too, huh?"

"Yeah, there will be lots of customers who come to see Mahiru."

"That's not what I mean, I'm talking about this."

"Just tell me what you mean."

"What I mean is, she'll probably be feeling uneasy because her own boyfriend is attracting so much attention. I bet you'd be real popular if you smiled like that all the time."

Ayaka poked his cheek with the clicker end of her pen. He casually knocked it away with a finger.

"In my opinion, I don't think I'm cut out to be popular or whatever."

"Fujimiya, listen, did you know this? It's a fact that humans first judge each other based on outward appearances. But your outward appearance doesn't just mean the features of your face. Cleanliness is a part of it, along with presence and how you carry yourself. Even facial expression is surprisingly important. It may be rude to say something like this, but if we were going just by faces, then there are definitely people who are more attractive than you, Fujimiya. But I don't think that that's the only thing that determines how likable you are."

"Well, I get what you're trying to say, and I think I agree."

When Amane had first gotten involved with Mahiru, he hadn't particularly had much liking for her. He had been aware that she was a beautiful girl, but he hadn't felt any affection toward her. Though a big part of that had also been that he'd had no particular interest in the opposite sex.

"In that case, you've got to agree that you could be popular, too. You look great when you smile," Ayaka said.

"No, it would be too conceited of me to agree to that."

"Ah-ha-ha! But it's true. You really do look better when you smile, you know. Though of course you're no match for my boyfriend!"

"Please, spare a thought for my feelings as you casually go on and on about your boyfriend," groaned Amane.

"Your complaining just makes me want to see him that much more."

"Hmm… Well, I guess that makes sense."

Ayaka was frank, cheerful, sociable, a good manager, and she understood Amane well after interacting with him for just a short while. He was curious to know about the boyfriend who had managed to charm a girl like her so completely. All he knew about the guy was that he was a good person and that he had a nice body.

"Well, you'll get there eventually. For now, you pass your customer service test. Full marks."

As proof that he had passed, Ayaka pulled a *hanamaru* flower sticker out of her apron and handed it to Amane.

Itsuki, who was watching from the side, had a sticker stuck on his forehead that said FAIL. It hadn't been stuck on him, though. He had gotten it from Ayaka and stuck it on himself.

The reason for Itsuki's failure had been because he had been acting foolish. He had received a cautionary warning not to smile so indecently.

"For now, I've got to watch the other folks handle their customers, so would you go over with Miss Shiina, Fujimiya?"

"…I'll do that."

"And speak to her with passionate words of love…"

"I will not do that."

He made his displeasure apparent with a look that asked *Who would do something like that in public*, and Ayaka brushed it off with her usual cheerful smile.

That took the wind out of his sails; so, feeling indescribably uneasy, Amane scratched at his cheek as he walked toward where Mahiru was.

"Mahiru?"

"Uh, ah, Amane..."

"Ah, it's the cause of Mahiru's head rush."

The head rush that Chitose mentioned must have been referring to the fact that Mahiru's cheeks were hot and flushed. Her normally pale cheeks had been rather colorful during his table service, too.

A maid with red cheeks and watery eyes was leaning back in her chair and looking up at him, which was incredibly bad for his heart.

"You know, Amane, you've got the 'Mahiru Killer' special trait, so you have to be careful!"

"What kind of special trait is that...?"

"A special attack ability that you only use on Mahiru?"

"...But I think that I'm not Amane's only target right now," Mahiru whispered.

Smiling wryly, Amane sat down next to her, and Mahiru practically swooned.

"Was I really that cool?"

"...Yes."

"Then I'm thankful to be your boyfriend... Now, you've just got to understand that I only have eyes for you, Mahiru."

"I—I know that, but...I guess I still have complicated feelings.

Mahiru was squirming and making herself smaller, as if she couldn't stand to be there. In an effort to soothe her, Amane stroked her head, and her face turned even redder.

"...I don't know if that was a special attack just for Mahiru, or if it was devastating in a wide area," Chitose speculated, "but by making

Mahiru embarrassed, you got like a multiplier effect, which is sure to wreak devastation."

"Did you say something?"

"Nope, not a thing."

Chitose had come out and said something strange, but when Amane shot her a pointed look, she averted her eyes, feigning innocence.

Chapter 7

Someone You Want to Invite

At Amane's school, the campus was not open to the public, not even during the culture festival. Only friends and family were able to attend, and even they needed to file applications beforehand. Tickets were distributed to students once they applied for them, and nonstudents used those tickets for entry. That was the system.

Of course, there was a limit on the number of tickets that any one student could request.

This measure was a reaction to a number of disturbances in recent years, including an incident several years earlier, in which a visitor had committed an act of violence on campus. Even during the culture festival, the students' safety was still the top priority, so the current policy had been decided upon after careful consideration.

"I don't suppose I have anyone to invite, do I?"

After dinner, Mahiru mumbled this like it was nothing out of the ordinary. She was gazing at one of the application forms that had been handed out in school.

Mahiru was often called an angel and was very popular, but it seemed she had never really made any particular close connections. It sounded like that had been the case during her middle school years as well, so there was no one whom she could call a good friend.

If she wasn't going to invite friends, the next option was family, but there was no way Mahiru could invite her parents. She wouldn't have wanted to invite her parents anyway, which must have led her to the conclusion that she had no one to invite.

"I don't have anybody close enough to want to go out of my way to invite, so I'll be on my own," Mahiru said. "Everyone I care about will already be at school, so I don't have to worry about it."

"Yeah, me too... Actually, if I don't say anything about this, my mom and dad will make a fuss..."

"Are your parents going to attend, too?"

"Last year I didn't mention it, and I got an earful afterward."

When his mother had found out, her pouting had been tremendous. She'd sent him a flurry of unhappy messages, and it had been bad enough that even Amane's father had called him to tell him how very sad he was making his mother.

From Amane's perspective, it had seemed too troublesome to invite them from so far away, and for something like a high school culture festival, it hadn't really seemed to make sense. Plus, he knew how his mother could get all touchy-feely even in public, and he didn't want people to think that he was such a mama's boy now that he was a high schooler. On top of all that, he also didn't want anyone to see how his parents flirted constantly.

As he might have expected, his mother was already aware that the culture festival was happening again, because she had already sent him a message that said, *"It's almost culture festival time, right?"* Without a doubt, that was her roundabout way of demanding a ticket.

Of course, Amane felt like he didn't have much of a choice, given what had happened the year before, but he was nevertheless reluctant to invite them.

"I'll invite them, I guess, with a reminder not to flirt in front of other people."

"Ah, ah-ha-ha."

Mahiru was perfectly aware of how naturally Amane's parents flirted with each other, so she was wearing a strained smile.

"Well, that means I'm only inviting two people, I guess," Amane said. "My hometown is far away, and I don't have any friends there who I'd want to invite anyway."

"Right…"

Mahiru, who knew a bit about the turmoil that Amane had experienced, and who had witnessed his farewell with a former friend, didn't seem like she was going to continue to say any more about it.

Amane was more worried about Mahiru, who had even more problems with her parents than he did.

As far as Amane had been able to determine, Mahiru's father, Asahi, was a pretty decent person, but it sounded like neither father nor daughter were inclined to see each other again. And Mahiru didn't seem to want to see her mother at all. Even Amane, who had only overheard the one conversation between the two of them, could tell that much. Her mother wasn't someone to invite to a culture festival.

Having said that, he didn't know everything about Mahiru's life before high school, so he didn't feel it was his place to say anything, but—

"That reminds me, you said you weren't going to invite anyone, Mahiru, but what about that housekeeper?"

Mahiru had been neglected by her parents, but Amane remembered that there had been a woman who had showered her with love and pretty much raised Mahiru herself.

The fact that Mahiru was so handy at housework and skilled at cooking was apparently thanks to the housekeeper's tutelage, and whenever Mahiru talked about the woman, she wore an affectionate expression. It would probably not be an exaggeration to say that, in a sense, the woman had acted as Mahiru's foster parent.

Amane's suggestion had clearly caught Mahiru by surprise because her eyes grew wide.

"You remembered Miss Koyuki? I think I only talked about her a little bit, though."

"You talked, so I listened. You don't want to invite her?"

"...I can't."

He'd thought it was a good suggestion, but Mahiru's face warped into a look of slight loneliness and sadness, which made him realize he had said the wrong thing.

"...Sorry."

Amane frowned, imagining she was about to tell him that something had happened to Miss Koyuki, the woman who had been her housekeeper, and that she couldn't just invite her. But Mahiru seemed aware of what he was imagining and waved her hand in a panic to dispel the thought.

"No, not like that! Miss Koyuki resigned as our housekeeper a little while after I started middle school... She, um, had back trouble."

"...Ah—"

"It may have been her job, but she was expected to manage a huge house all by herself. She was forced to work too hard. I still feel bad thinking back on it."

Once Amane heard that she had strained her back, he understood why it would be impossible for her to continue.

Once someone injured their back, even if it healed, it was easy to injure it again.

It was like going through life with a bomb in your lower back. She would have been unable to do any heavy labor, there was no way she could take the risk.

Amane could imagine how it might be impossible for someone in such a condition to go on an outing, and he understood perfectly well why Mahiru was hesitant.

"She's living now with her daughter and her daughter's husband. Even if I did get her to come, I would worry about her physical condition. There aren't too many easy resting spots for visitors to use, and we're some distance from where she lives anyway, so I would feel bad even inviting her."

"Gotcha. That's a real shame."

"Yeah."

He could tell by looking at her facial expression that Mahiru adored her former housekeeper.

Amane would have liked to meet the person who had been so involved not only in teaching Mahiru her life skills, but in shaping her personality, and he would have liked to thank her. But if she was in poor health, then there wasn't a lot they could do.

"I'm a little disappointed, too. It's too bad I won't be able to say hello to her, even though she's the one who worked so hard to take care of you. I wonder if I ought to go introduce myself one of these days."

"Huh, i-introduce yourself?"

"Yeah. She's like a parent to you, right?"

He was just guessing, but the housekeeper had played a great part in shaping Mahiru.

Amane felt he owed a great debt to the person whose attitude and behavior was more parental than her parents, and who had taught Mahiru many things. If she hadn't been there, Mahiru might not have grown up so well, and might never have connected with Amane.

"…Yes, she is."

"Then I need to meet her, don't I?"

He had basically declared to her real father that he was going to be courting his daughter, and her father had accepted it. But Amane figured he ought to say something to the parental figure who had actually raised her.

As far as he had heard from Mahiru, the woman had taken remarkable care of her, going above and beyond her professional duties to shower Mahiru with affection. So Amane felt it would be wrong to take her hand without getting approval from the person who he owed such a great debt of gratitude.

In any case, he felt like he wanted to meet the person who had raised his girlfriend, face-to-face, and tell her directly of his intentions.

"Well, let's think about it a little further down the line, once things are more settled, shall we? It would also be rude to visit out of the blue, so I would want to wait for the right time and make an appointment. You seem to know where to reach her, so you could write, or call first...uh, Mahiru?"

Since he intended to romance the girl who was basically like her daughter, he reasoned that he needed to formally introduce himself, and he was thinking of the best way to do that.

But Mahiru, the girl in question, was peering around the room awkwardly.

"N-no, it's nothing!"

"That's not what your face says."

"It's nothing."

Mahiru didn't seem inclined to say anything further. Instead, she pressed her favorite cushion into his face, blinding him, so Amane smiled resignedly and let her do as she pleased.

Chapter 8

The Scene Right Before the Culture Festival

Running a café for the culture festival required a lot of time and labor, but things were proceeding much better than Amane had imagined they would. They'd gotten someone to loan them the costumes, and that had probably been the biggest hurdle.

After overcoming that major obstacle, they had to figure out the interior design and decide on what they were going to serve to customers. Utilizing the desks and chairs in the classroom, they had managed to make the space look quite nice, so that was no problem. But their concerns about what food and drinks they were going to serve was more difficult. The culture festival lasted for two days, so they would have to skillfully anticipate and prepare enough food to last while also being careful about sanitation.

However, it was not going to be that difficult. After considering the food safety angle, and the problem of labor, the class had decided to purchase large amounts of premade food that they would then serve.

The class was putting on a café staffed by maids and butlers. The main draw was basically going to be enjoying the appearance of the staff and the overall atmosphere, so they felt compelled to compromise on the refreshments, which was the right call.

Once they considered the number of classes on standby that had applied to use the home economics room, their decision to offer pre-made food was set.

"Well, we're kind of going all out on the drinks, though."

Itsuki, their festival chairman, made this declaration with a cheerful wink and a playful smile. He was clearly in high spirits as he slapped a bag full of ground coffee beans.

For the coffee, Itsuki had relied on a special connection. A specialist shop had agreed to sell him the coffee for a bargain price.

Really, it was better to grind them as needed, but as one might expect, that wouldn't be possible given the labor and facilities at a snack bar run by high school students. So they had ended up doing it in advance. The tea leaves for brewing the tea had also been fully prepared, and when it came to their other menu offerings, they were all ready to go.

"This came together better than I expected," Chitose mumbled quietly while looking around at the classroom. It was in the final stages of decoration.

The interior of their café was fundamentally a school classroom, so there was a limit to what they could do, but the tablecloths and cushions they used to disguise the desks, combined with the little decorations they had left on the tops of the lockers, produced the right atmosphere.

By no means would anyone mistake it for a real café, but it was perfectly sufficient for a student exhibition. After all, the main attraction would be the students wearing their costumes.

"It sure did. I think we've managed to do enough."

"I think you're right. It looks totally different with the curtains and the little decorations."

"Everyone did a really good job. This looks right."

Pointing at the extravagant curtains with their decorative gold cords that they had borrowed from the drama club, Chitose mumbled quietly, "We'll be in trouble if we get them dirty, though."

They hadn't set up too many seats right next to the curtains, but on the off chance that they got dirty, it would probably be expensive to have them professionally cleaned.

"Well, I think we've done enough here. All we have to do now is hope that customers come by."

"…I have a feeling we're gonna be slammed during the time slot when Miss Shiina is working as a maid," Itsuki said. "In fact, we'll probably get packed with people trying to see her."

"My girlfriend isn't a piece of bait," Amane replied. "Besides, the other girls also look great in their costumes, so I think it's rude to say everyone will be coming just for Mahiru."

Although Amane was only interested in Mahiru, looking at things objectively, all of the girls wearing the maid costumes were good-looking, and their outfits suited them well. Sure, even if he hadn't been biased, Mahiru was particularly adorable, and she did stand out from the crowd, but she certainly wasn't the only one who looked good.

"Itsuki, I think you'd do well to follow the example of what Amane just said."

"Ow, owww, you're cute, too, Chi!"

"It sounds so shallow! If you don't give me more compliments, your penalty is to treat me to the afternoon tea course at the place I told you about earlier."

"But that place is so expensive!"

"I've heard they really do have one butler per table, so you can watch and learn!"

"The cost of that lesson is too high, in more ways than one!"

Leaving his two friends arguing happily and planning out the details of their date, Amane turned to Mahiru, who was sitting quietly beside him.

For some reason, Mahiru was wearing a complicated expression on her face.

"Mahiru?"

"…Amane, do you think…d-do you think that I'm the cutest girl here?"

"What's this all of a sudden? Are you worried because I complimented the other girls just now? …I don't know how to answer such an obvious question. In my eyes, you're the best-looking. And the cutest."

"O-okay."

To Amane, it was a given that Mahiru was special. But she still seemed to be worried about it. She was apparently feeling a little bit jealous.

When Amane praised Mahiru directly, in a low voice, those few words seemed to be enough for her to understand his feelings because her lips spread into a broad smile, and she looked very happy.

They were in school, so she couldn't cling to him, but she bashfully grabbed a little handful of his sleeve. Even that gesture drew some attention from the other students, so this time it was Amane who found himself harboring complicated feelings in his heart because of how adorable his girlfriend was.

…*She's going to attract even more looks on the actual day, huh?*

At the moment, they were only getting unenthusiastic looks from their classmates, which wasn't so bad.

The real problem would be the actual culture festival.

Amane was expecting that they would have to deal with people giving her rude looks; people who had no manners at all.

I'll try not to be apart from her, as best I can.

Feeling privately grateful that Itsuki and the others had assigned them the same shift for exactly that reason, he looked back and forth between Mahiru, who was wearing a bashful smile on her face, and Itsuki and Chitose, who looked like they were getting along well even as they argued. Watching them made him break into a little smile.

Chapter 9

Culture Festival, Day One

The day of the actual culture festival was blessed with clear weather.

The lingering notes of summer had been fading bit by bit. Fortunately, the temperature that day was pleasant, and it seemed like overheating would not be a problem, even though their costumes were much heavier than normal clothes. Amane was happy that he wouldn't be sweating, even with his necktie tightly fastened.

"It's a little nerve-racking being on the very first shift, isn't it?"

"Well, we'll swap out in the afternoon, so we've got to try our best until then. You're both here, Kadowaki and Mahiru, so it seems like it's going to be really crowded."

"Sorry about that. But, you know there's no helping it, so I guess I've already given up."

They'd finished sitting through the opening ceremony for the students that was always held in the gym before the festival. Amane was chatting with Yuuta, who was on shift with him, as they got changed in the waiting room that they were using in place of a locker room, but…Yuuta was already smiling in a disinterested way about the whole thing.

Being something of a spectacle seemed to be an everyday

occurrence for him; the only difference was the clothing, so it sounded like he intended to give up and accept it.

Without meaning to, Amane gave his friend a pitying glance, thinking about how good looks really did bring unceasing troubles. But when Yuuta noticed Amane's expression, he smiled a little.

"You'd better be careful, too, Fujimiya. Miss Shiina will be burning with jealousy."

"Nobody will notice me while you're there, Kadowaki. I'll just stand quietly in the background, so it'll be fine."

"So you say… Well, you'll probably have more to be jealous of than she will, huh, Fujimiya?"

"Never mind burning with jealousy, I'm already feeling a chill of anxiety."

Mahiru was adorable, and her maid costume looked great on her. It looked so incredible that he was worried about some strange man following her around or sexually harassing her.

He knew that there would probably also be a lot of students visiting the café to see Mahiru, which, as her boyfriend, he did not especially appreciate. He was mainly worried that they might give her some impolite looks.

Yuuta seemed to have guessed what was in Amane's heart. With a friendly smile, he said, "Good luck," and patted him on the back.

They finished changing and headed for the classroom where their classmates were assembling after finishing most of the final preparations. The students who weren't there were probably off working in the kitchen.

Itsuki, who was still in his school uniform because his shift was in the afternoon, checked that his classmates were all gathered, then stood in front of the teacher's lectern wearing his usual cheerful grin.

"Today is the first day of the culture festival. Honestly, I have no idea how many people are coming. It's not like we've ever tried this before, but what it comes down to is that we've got some really popular folks in our class."

Itsuki glanced over at Yuuta and Mahiru.

Both of them were wearing smiled awkwardly. They had probably prepared themselves for the worst.

"Well, let's go out and do things our way," Itsuki continued. "It'll be a waste if we don't enjoy this precious culture festival. Whether any customers come or not, it doesn't matter. To be blunt, I don't think we'll have this kind of time and energy next year. Second year is the best time to enjoy everything to the fullest. We'll all be preoccupied worrying about exams next year, I bet."

"People are going to get depressed if you say stuff like that!"

"I feel all gloomy all of a sudden."

"Sorry, sorry! Okay, no more serious talk! Let's go out and have fun at the culture festival again this year!"

For a moment, a melancholy feeling ran through the class, but with Itsuki's smile, the atmosphere instantly grew cheerful again. It had been the right call for Itsuki to act as their leader.

"Oh, right, right, I have a business matter, or like, an important point to note. I think you all already know this, but we're enforcing a no photos policy in the café. I'll ask everyone to verbally remind guests at reception, but all photography is banned. Even if someone asks, you have to refuse. Tell them we don't offer that service. It'll only cause headaches, okay?"

Of course, they were not offering any photo-taking services, such as the kind often found at the special cafés that existed in the electronics district in the center of the city. Ultimately, this was a student culture festival, and they weren't in the business of selling the likeness of their classmates.

To that end, they had posters stuck up in the café prohibiting photographs, and a word about it on the side of the menus that were set out on the tables.

Similarly, video recording was prohibited on campus throughout the culture festival event. Apparently, there had been a stalking incident against some girls at another school after the students there streamed their events online, so recordings of any kind had been banned at Amane's school for the past few years.

When Amane thought about the fact that the world had changed so much that they needed to ban such things, he got restless. He felt both impressed and disgusted by technology. At any rate, there were bound to be some people who didn't follow the rules, so they all had to be on their guard.

"Well, that about does it for the warnings. Things'll be picking up before too long."

The same moment that Itsuki finished talking, the loudspeaker in the classroom played a quiet tone, and then the principal began reading announcements about the culture festival's events.

"All right, let's do our best today and tomorrow, guys! We're aiming to be the class with the highest sales!"

Itsuki pumped his fist in the air as he shouted loudly and a little impulsively, and excitement rippled through the class. The students were plenty fired up.

Amane also straightened up again, and Mahiru, who had been standing quietly by his side listening, smiled demurely and murmured, "Let's do our best."

As everyone could have predicted, they had customers from the moment they opened...mainly other students, who had flocked to Amane's classroom.

"The angel effect is scary," muttered one of their classmates, another boy who was in charge of customer service on the same shift as Amane, named Yamazaki.

Perhaps he was overwhelmed by the unusual spectacle of a student exhibition having every seat filled from the very start of the festival. Or it might be more accurate to say that he was overwhelmed by the enthusiasm of the clientele.

Naturally enough, there was no way that their café could handle all of the customers at once, so they were limiting the number of people who could come in at one time. But even so, it was no surprise that some of the students were caught off guard by the level of success.

Every time Mahiru walked down an aisle, she drew stares from all the boys. Amane's face was threatening to twist into a combined expression of astonishment, admiration, and annoyance.

He understood the situation perfectly well and had resigned himself to endure it, but still, an unpleasant situation was an unpleasant situation. From Mahiru's perspective, she could probably say the same thing about Amane, so both of them probably felt the same way.

"Well, this is exactly what we expected. Anyway, we have another customer."

In a chiding tone, Yamazaki left to show a customer who had just entered the café to her seat.

It was the duty of any staff who weren't busy to receive the customers, but some were trying to request particular servers, which was an issue. They weren't offering a choice, and Amane thought that anybody who wanted something like that ought to go visit a real maid café.

The female student who was being shown in just then had probably come hoping to see Yuuta, but at the moment Yuuta was looking after a different customer, so she would have to make do with Amane. He felt a little apologetic.

"Please have a seat, Miss."

Amane pulled out a chair and turned to his customer with the smile Ayaka had taught him. The female student, who had been looking a little disappointed, stared at him in apparent surprise.

Feeling guilty that he obviously wasn't the person she'd been hoping for, he showed her where the basket for her bag was and then placed a menu in front of her.

"Our recommended item of the day is this A set. How does that sound, Miss?"

"S-sure, I'll have that…"

Although Amane had given his recommendation, the menu actually consisted only of three sets, each combining a baked dessert and a drink. It would have caused issues if people had only ordered individual beverages, so they had decided to sell sets instead.

When it came to allergies, the students at reception were advising guests to disclose any restrictions ahead of time, so that shouldn't be a problem.

To the girl who had placed her order with some hesitation, Amane answered, "Very well. Please wait here until the items you've ordered are ready." Then he bowed once with polite movements and went to tell the people working in the back.

"One A set. We're getting lots of orders, so hang in there, guys."

In the back, Amane's classmates were arranging sweets onto plates and going back and forth between the classroom and the section of the school kitchen that their class had reserved. One classmate who happened to be free for a second raised his head sluggishly.

"Whoa…I just looked at reception, it's crazy."

"Never say die," Amane encouraged him.

"We'll get through it somehow, since we prepared most of the things for our café before we even opened, but man…"

"We'll get through it, but…"

"…Looking out there, I'm thinking you guys are going to have it rough later."

"Oh yeah? Well, Kadowaki's really in demand, and I do think we're only going to get busier."

"That's not what I mean, though."

The other student sighed at him, but didn't say specifically what he was alluding to. Amane didn't really understand, but he figured it wasn't that big of a deal.

He gave his classmate a look that said he didn't understand what he meant and got a pitying look in return.

"Also, every time Miss Shiina's come to the back, she's had kind of an unhappy look on her face."

"What, every time?"

"I think it was because of you."

"I'm stuck serving customers, there's nothing I can do."

"That's also true, but that's probably not the issue."

"I have no idea what you've been trying to say this whole time."

Amane got the feeling that he was somehow being blamed for something in a roundabout way, but he couldn't quite grasp what. He frowned.

He figured that it was probably Mahiru being jealous, but from the way the other boy was speaking, it sounded like she might be sulking for some other reason.

He decided to ask Mahiru about it later, cut off the conversation there, and carried the order to his table.

An hour had passed since they had opened up shop, but there was no sign of their customers losing interest. If anything, it was growing.

There had been a steady increase in the number of guests, and the fact that they were waiting in line seemed to be stirring up people's curiosity. At first their customers had mostly been students, but gradually they started seeing more outside invitees.

Though they understandably didn't show the same level of excitement as the students, here and there Amane could see customers swooning at the appearance of the staff, who were all attractive young people.

Among them, he also saw some relatively young customers trying to strike up friendly conversations with the staff, but they were getting the cold shoulder.

"You're awfully cute, young lady."

Mahiru was of course also receiving compliments, but she thanked the customers with a reserved smile and went right back to her job.

She interrupted the man who was trying to make a pass at her, making it clear that she had no intention of allowing him to continue the conversation, and instead repeated her question.

"Have you decided what you'd like to order?"

She sounded like she was reminding him that he was just another customer, and the way she handled him was the same as anyone else.

"I have decided on my order, but more importantly, you…"

"If you've decided, then I can take your order."

"Um, so after this, if you're free—"

"I'm terribly sorry, but we don't offer those sorts of services. If you've decided, then I can take your order."

The man was still trying to persuade her, but Mahiru handled him by the book, smiling all the while. He seemed to realize that he was getting cold looks from the other staff members and, looking deflated, he meekly gave her his order.

That kind of thing happened multiple times, leaving Amane wearing a lopsided smile.

…*Looks like it's not just me. Everyone seems to be feeling overprotective.*

He sensed that the whole class was working together to keep Mahiru from facing any danger.

He knew, of course, that she was beloved by their class, but he hadn't expected her to warrant so much consideration.

"I know that you're worried, but the rest of us are keeping an eye out, too, so try not to be too tense, okay?"

Amane was secretly marveling at their kindness when Yuuta approached him with a wry smile, apparently free for a moment.

Girls had been approaching Yuuta all day, but perhaps because he was used to it, Amane had seen him dodging their advances smoothly.

"I understand that it makes you uneasy, having such a popular girlfriend, but even you can't be worrying about Miss Shiina constantly, Fujimiya. The rest of us will support you whenever we can."

"Kadowaki…"

It was at times like this that Amane really appreciated the kind nature of Yuuta and his other classmates. Gradually, the warmth of that feeling permeated his chest.

"Well, I don't want my friend feeling bad, that's part of it, but…I also don't want anyone to cause problems when you're finally healing."

"Healing?"

"The consensus of the class seems to be: Don't pop their sweet little bubble. No one wants to get in your way."

"Sorry, I don't really get your meaning."

Amane didn't think anyone would blame him for looking at Yuuta with eyes that said *What the heck are you talking about?*

He had never known his friend Yuuta to say anything like that, and he didn't understand exactly what he meant, either. Amane stiffened, and Yuuta smiled broadly and chuckled in apparent amusement.

"Well, I think I can just say one way or another, that Miss Shiina is loved. I think I can also say that people approve of you two going out together."

"So you're basically saying we're under observation?"

"Well, I mean, the two of you are always flirting, so people do see that."

"We are not always flirting."

"Oh, come on."

Yuuta turned the same skeptical look back on him.

Amane pursed his lips.

He didn't remember flirting intentionally.

He didn't remember doing it, but he did sometimes touch Mahiru without thinking about it. And it had probably come across that way many times.

...I've got to be careful.

Otherwise, he might unintentionally mess up some time.

Yuuta saw that Amane had fallen silent. With an amused chuckle, he said nonchalantly, "Well, I guess it's all good as long as the two of you are happy."

That embarrassed Amane somewhat, and he pressed his lips closed even tighter than before.

"Amane?"

Amane stepped into the back for a moment, and Mahiru, who also happened to be in the back, approached him, her eyes beaming enthusiastically.

Feeling his heart throb at her sincere smile, the one she only turned on for Amane and completely different from her customer service smile, he turned and greeted her with his own smile that he had reserved for Mahiru only.

"You're not too tired?" he asked.

"I'm fine. Everyone's being so thoughtful...though I was surprised to see everyone smiling even while they intimidated the people who try to photograph us."

"Ah. Well, there's already signs that photographs are prohibited, and they're telling people upfront. If someone ignores all that, then we've got no other choice."

"Somehow, everyone seems very motivated…"

"I guess so."

Amane couldn't say that it was because everyone was, for some reason, watching out for them, so he didn't give a straight answer. Mahiru didn't seem to notice and giggled slightly, in a voice like a tinkling bell.

He wasn't sure whether she didn't realize it, or if she was just used to it, but for the time being, Mahiru seemed to be preoccupied with the café. She glanced around at the back of the house.

"The customers are coming in more consistently than I expected, don't you think?"

"Yeah, I guess it's the bandwagon effect or something. The thing where you see people lined up, so you want to go in."

"Probably, yeah. Of course, there's also the other thing."

Then she shifted her gaze to Amane.

"…I think that people come in if there's someone here they want to see," she said. "Listening to the conversations out there, I've heard a lot of that."

"Well, if you're talking about the students, it does seem like a lot of them would come to see you, Mahiru…"

"…Amane, there are a number of things I need to discuss with you once this culture festival is over."

"Huh, like what?"

"A number of things."

Mahiru frowned slightly, as if she was feeling dissatisfied about something, but hiding it. Worried that he had tripped some kind of land mine, Amane gazed into Mahiru's eyes, and she turned away in a huff.

However, this didn't seem to be a signal that she was angry, but rather a gesture that came from embarrassment. Her cheeks were faintly tinged with red.

"…It's not fair, you looking like that."

"Huh…it's about time you got used to it. How many times did you see me like this during practice?"

"The way you look at others and the way you look at me is just too different. It's impossible to get used to it."

"Well then we're both in trouble…"

The looks they gave their sweethearts and the looks they gave their customers weren't supposed to be the same. Even if an incredibly cute female customer came in, Amane would treat her the same as all the others.

And anyway, he didn't think he would ever meet a person who could rival Mahiru's cuteness. He thought she looked more adorable than anyone else in the world, wearing a sulky, embarrassed expression; the kind that she would only show to Amane.

"You just don't get it, Amane… I won't hand you over just because they finally realized how good you are."

When Mahiru suddenly changed the topic, Amane cocked his head, wondering what she was talking about all of a sudden. But she didn't say anything further, she just slapped her hand against his chest once, as if venting her anger.

The thing that gave Amane the most anxiety about Mahiru working in the café at the culture festival was not that she attracted such attention. And it was not the people who pestered her trying to strike up a conversation because of her good looks.

It was the arrival of a person who would try to abuse someone else to satisfy one of the major three desires of human beings.

Just after noon, less than an hour before Amane and Mahiru's shift was over—

*   *   *

There was a male customer who, from the moment he entered the room, had not stopped following the female staff with his eyes. Of course, at this café many customers were there to be waited on by good-looking girls, so that wasn't unusual.

However, this customer had been looking at them like he was sizing them up, so Amane had a feeling that they needed to be a little cautious around him.

Amane had just finished delivering a customer's order and was heading back to the back room with a tray in one hand…when he saw someone else's hand reach out for Mahiru.

Mahiru had also just finished delivering an order to that man. The moment she turned around was when it happened. It went without saying that she couldn't see what was happening behind her.

Amane saw him trying to touch her lower back, which was covered by her skirt—actually, his hand was headed for her rear end.

Amane took one step forward. Because he was so nearby, Amane was able to reach out with a relatively relaxed movement, using what he was holding in his hand.

"Sir, we must ask that you refrain from careless contact with the staff in this establishment."

Amane had been able to slip his tray between the man's hand and Mahiru's body before there was any contact. He quietly spoke words of caution, feigning a gentle tone the whole time.

The expression on his face was genial, but on the inside, he felt like he was on fire. Even under normal circumstances, he would get a little irritated if he saw someone hitting on his adorable girlfriend, but that man had tried to grope her.

Mahiru turned around at the sound of his voice and seemed to understand implicitly from the positions of the hand and the tray what had almost happened to her. Her face twitched in surprise as she took a step back.

Amane, who had slipped in to protect Mahiru, was wearing the gentlest smile he could muster.

Once everyone noticed what was happening, the café fell silent. Amane felt everyone's gazes gathering on them, but he was so angry that he didn't care.

However, at the same time, he was calm.

He had only witnessed a failed attempt, something that the culprit would have been able to explain away if he tried.

The people around them probably realized that, too. They were staring at the man's hand, but he hadn't done anything yet. If the man were to say that it was an accident, Amane would likely have no option but to back down.

But Amane realized there was one thing the man could not explain away, even if he claimed that he was innocent of trying to touch Mahiru.

"By the way, sir, where is your ticket for admission onto campus?"

He saw the man's eyes go wide at the sudden change of subject.

"Allow me to ask you this question: How did you enter the school grounds? You don't seem to have an admission wristband."

At their school, visitors were given disposable, yet sturdy, wristbands to wear, showing they were allowed on campus.

There had been a lot of disturbing incidents in recent years, as well as a rash of thefts, so during this culture festival period, when a great many people were coming and going, the students didn't even wear their name tags, but had lanyards hanging from their necks with cords color coded by school year, and ordinary visitors wore the wristbands.

Inside the school, there were some staging areas for the students that outsiders were not permitted to enter. This was also a measure taken to ensure that no one slipped behind the scenes.

When Amane pointed that out, the man stammered, "I-it got wet and tore off, so…"

Amane smiled even wider. "How strange. But it was made of waterproof paper. Also, I believe it should say in your pamphlet that if you lose your wristband, you are supposed to report it to the main office, because they can issue you a new one. By the way, who is the student who applied for you to have permission to come on campus? What is their school year and class number? I'm sure you can tell me that."

"W-well, I—"

"…It's no use asking, is it?"

Amane put his smile away, and looked over to the café staff who were watching this all go down.

"Sorry, but would someone go call a member of the student council or a teacher? I'm sure it's unwise to have uninvited outsiders wandering around."

"We've already contacted someone, and it sounds like the teacher who is patrolling the festival is on the way."

"Great, thank you."

Amane shrugged with a sense of relief at the quick response and initiative from Kadowaki, then turned his attention back to the attempted groper with a smile.

Of course, he was aware that his eyes were not smiling.

"Sir. Without even mentioning your conduct a moment ago, it is an issue to have unrelated persons enter campus without permission. I'm terribly sorry, but I believe they will want to speak with you in the main office."

In a detached tone, he told the man what was going to happen. Just as he finished, the homeroom teacher arrived and approached the man. Amane took Mahiru, who had been standing off to the side, by the hand and pulled her away, breathing a quiet sigh.

The attempted groping would be reported, and likely result in the forced eviction of the culprit. Some of the guys he had served earlier hadn't seemed to understand why the school had implemented the advance application process, and their foolishness had astounded Amane.

The applications noted which students had invited which guests, mainly to ensure that no strangers were invited.

A guest could be identified if they got out of hand, and the student who had invited them could also be taken to task, so common sense dictated that hardly anybody would act in an inappropriate way.

Although, hitting on the girls was just barely on the safe side. So as long as someone wasn't too persistent, they weren't likely to be admonished.

Amane was concerned about how the man had gotten onto campus, but he assumed they would interrogate him in the main office.

Next year, or possibly even the very next day, people would probably be obligated to present their wristbands for identification before entering their café.

The man was saying something, but it didn't have anything to do with Amane, so he ignored it.

When Amane confirmed that the man had left the classroom with their homeroom teacher, he looked back at his customer with a smile, as if nothing had happened.

"My dear customers, I'm so sorry for the disturbance. Please go ahead and enjoy your tea."

He bowed gracefully and the other staff followed suit and bowed, too, as if to reassure everyone that the disturbance was over.

Amane made sure that he heard people start chatting again, as they had been before. Then without a word, he took Mahiru's hand once again and pulled her toward the back.

"Eh, uh, Amane?"

"We're almost at the shift change anyway, so go ahead and start your break first. If you wait for me in the back, I'll be there soon to get changed with you."

When he looked at all of the other students surrounding them, assuming they would have no problem with that, his classmates all waved as if to say, 'hurry up and go', so he bowed his head a little bit, took Mahiru into the back, and sat her down in a chair that was there.

He stroked Mahiru's head, noting that she was a little out of it, like she hadn't yet shaken off the shock of it all. He reasoned that even if they were on the cusp of a shift change, they couldn't both abandon the floor, so he headed for the front again.

When it was time for the shift change, Amane headed to the back, where he found Mahiru still sitting in her chair, looking very small and waiting quietly. In her hand was a paper cup full of coffee, which a thoughtful classmate must have given her to help calm her down.

Mahiru noticed that Amane had come back, and the look in her eyes softened with relief. When he saw that, Amane's eyes also softened.

"Welcome back," Mahiru said.

"Thanks. Have you calmed down?"

"...It really wasn't bad enough for everyone to be worrying about me."

"Of course they're worried. That's normal."

He had pulled her into the back because he'd had a hunch that it was taking her time to process what happened, and he didn't think his judgment had been in error.

Mahiru looked just a little bit uneasy. He tried stroking her head again, and she cast her eyes downward bashfully and sipped her coffee to try to hide her feelings.

When Amane saw that the contents of the paper cup were gone, he laid his sweatshirt, which he had left in the back, over Mahiru's lap.

Their school had a central air conditioning system that always maintained a suitable temperature, but as the seasons transitioned into autumn, it was getting colder little by little, so many students carried jackets with them. This time, Amane had brought his sweatshirt, thinking he would get Mahiru to put it on.

"Here, put this on. You know you'll stand out if you walk around in those clothes."

If Mahiru went out walking around still dressed as a maid, she would attract attention, and outside of their café, still photography was generally allowed, so Amane was ready with the sweatshirt, so that she wouldn't cause too much of an uproar.

Because of the difference in their heights, Amane's sweatshirt covered Mahiru down to the thighs, so if she took off her apron, she probably wouldn't stand out all that much. Mahiru herself always attracted attention, so there was no helping the fact that her beauty would draw people's eyes.

Once Mahiru removed her apron, obediently put on the sweatshirt that she had been handed, and had zipped the front all the way up to the top, she somehow seemed to be in a better mood than she had been a moment earlier.

As she worked very hard to roll up the overlong sleeves, she brought her nose close to the fabric and sniffed loudly, her lips spreading into an open, broad smile. Amane wished she would stop doing that. Her warm smile was hard on his heart.

Witnessing their interaction, Itsuki, who was about to start his afternoon shift, grinned broadly as he straightened out his necktie, so Amane frowned hard, which made him grin even more.

✳   ✳   ✳

Amane felt as if he had somehow been defeated, and put on an even more sullen face, but Mahiru then batted her eyes and smiled again, so he reluctantly accepted the stares.

That said, it wasn't like he wanted to continue drawing attention, so Amane pulled the bag that contained his usual school uniform from his personal locker in the back. If he took off his jacket and waistcoat first and left them in the locker, he figured he wouldn't stand out walking down the hallways.

He knew that Mahiru was going to change, too, so he stood up and put her apron in the locker, then took out her uniform.

"All right, we're out," he said to Itsuki. "Good luck for the rest of the afternoon."

"Roger! Go flirt to your hearts' content."

"Shut up. And make sure you two aren't flirting inside the café."

He frowned again at the flippant answer, but Mahiru squeezed his hand, so he couldn't really scowl any more than that, and with a terribly twisted expression, Amane left the classroom with Mahiru.

When they stepped into the hallway, they could see, as expected, that it was quite a bit livelier than usual. Even with the advance application system, a great many guests had turned up, so the crowd was hardly surprising. But the hallways, which usually weren't so noisy, were crowded and a little bit uncomfortable.

"So many people," he remarked.

"Apparently more guests were invited than usual."

"Well, if there are this many folks here, I guess that explains how that weird guy also slipped past the front desk."

Amane had heard that their culture festival had a bigger budget than the festivals at other schools, so the scale was quite large. That was probably also why there were a fair number of outsiders who wanted to attend.

When Amane mentioned the weird guy, Mahiru's gaze fell. Amane realized that he shouldn't have said that, and he squeezed her hand a little harder.

"…You okay?" he asked.

"Ah, y-yes. It startled me, but it was a failed attempt, so…"

Mahiru seemed to realize that he was worried about her, and she quickly shook her head, but if she were really fine, he didn't think she would have been making that face.

"Sorry, I should have been watching more closely."

"You were busy, too, Amane. Anyway, I wasn't paying attention, that's what caused it…"

"It doesn't matter whether you were paying attention or not, guys like that will always try something. That's why the rest of us have to look out and keep them away."

Whether she was paying attention or not, some things were out of her control. And anyway, there was simply no excuse for a vile offense like groping.

Mahiru seemed to be blaming herself for her own carelessness, but there was no way that it was her fault in any way. The kind of people who would do those sorts of things would do them no matter what.

"It's not your fault, Mahiru. The idea that attractive people should expect to be victimized is pure nonsense. Everyone deserves respect, regardless of gender."

"…Yeah."

"So don't try to blame yourself," he whispered gently.

Mahiru frowned, looking just a little troubled, then pressed her body closely against Amane's arm.

"…I don't want to be touched by anyone else. Not when you still haven't touched me that much, Amane."

Mahiru's voice trembled a little as she whispered quietly, so he squeezed her hand back to comfort her.

They were doing this as they walked around, so they were getting some bothersome looks from the people around them. But it was well-known throughout the school that Amane was dating the angel, so it was much too late to care. Amane himself was still uncomfortable with being looked at, but he was used to it by now.

"You said I haven't done it much, but I feel like actually I've hardly done it at all."

"Sometimes when I come to wake you up, you flail at me when you're still asleep."

"Stop me when I do that, would you? It makes me seem perverted."

When this shocking fact came to light, Amane stared at Mahiru, and saw that the vitality appeared to have come back into her face. She had been looking somewhat dejected, but now she was wearing an impish smile.

"I don't think touching your girlfriend's body is perverted, though."

"Even so, I mean…"

"I really don't mind it."

"You probably should, at least a little. I'll definitely touch you."

"Don't you want to touch me?"

"Well yeah, I am a guy, so I want to touch you all over, but it's still too early for that."

Of course he wanted to touch her, but Amane was well aware that a man's self-control was a fragile thing, so he had been trying not to touch her any more than was necessary.

He was certain that Mahiru did not dislike his touch.

If anything, she liked it when Amane touched her. She said that it was pleasant to share their body heat, and also that it made her happy when he touched her.

However, if Amane were to touch her the way he really wanted to touch her, things would likely escalate, so he had to hold himself back.

Whether or not she understood his state of mind, when Amane suddenly turned away, Mahiru chuckled softly and clung tightly to his arm.

"Please, I need you to understand that I don't dislike it."

"...I know that."

Even though he knew that she granted him that permission because she liked him, it was bad for his heart to hear her say it again.

Deciding secretly in his heart that once he was able to take responsibility for anything that might happen, he would be all over her, Amane stroked the palm of Mahiru's hand in a tickling way, and she smiled happily at his side.

Chapter 10

Going Around the Culture Festival with the Angel

After changing back into their school uniforms and storing their costumes in their lockers, Amane and Mahiru walked around the school, figuring they ought to tour the culture festival.

It was a little bit past lunchtime, but the refreshment booths selling food and drinks were still doing brisk business. Many of the students were also changing shifts around that time, so the booths were actually probably even busier than before.

Amane had also been working hard in the unfamiliar business of customer service, so he wanted to wander around the school and pick out whatever he felt like eating, but…as he probably should have expected, Mahiru stood out.

Here and there, he heard voices remarking that she was the maid from the café, so it was safe to say that their class café was popular. He was glad that so many people had come by.

Amane was uncomfortable hearing people whisper about Mahiru, but she had resigned herself to it, or rather, she ignored it as a matter of course, so he decided not to worry about it too much, either.

"What do you want to eat, Mahiru?"

"Let me see… Something that I don't usually eat would be nice, I think."

"Something you don't usually eat, huh? …Like yakisoba, or takoyaki?"

It wasn't that they never made yakisoba, but since Mahiru didn't like foods with strong flavors all that much, if they did make yakisoba, it would only be seasoned with some salt or maybe with a basic sauce. When it came to takoyaki, they didn't even have the equipment to make it at home.

They almost never ate out, and they rarely had the chance to eat festival foods.

Since it was a rare opportunity, Amane decided he wanted to eat yakisoba with a flavorful sauce, and he started walking toward one of the food stalls. But on the way, he heard some familiar voices coming from the stairwell.

They were coming from the stairs that led up to the roof. Thinking that the roof access ought to be closed off, Amane went up the stairs a little way, and when he looked at the landing…there were some classmates with whom he had recently become acquainted with.

"Oh, Fujimiya and Shiina?"

Amane blinked in surprise to see Ayaka, who had called their names in a curious tone of voice.

There were hardly any places to sit inside the school, so he wasn't surprised by the fact that she was there, but…he was surprised by the position she was in.

Next to Ayaka was a male student with his cheeks stuffed with yakisoba, and Ayaka was cuddled up close to him, with her hand right under his chin. It looked like she was trying to make sure he didn't drop any noodles.

"…What are you doing in a place like this?"

"Huh? Just what it looks like. Eating, we're eating. Look, Sou sweetie, it's Fujimiya, the guy I mentioned earlier."

"Mm."

The male student looked at Amane and made a muffled sound of acknowledgement with his mouth full. Then he gulped down his yakisoba… Or at least he tried, but maybe because it was so sudden, he frowned, and pounded on his chest.

As if she had expected that to happen, Ayaka handed him a bottle of tea. "It's because you don't chew properly," she scolded.

After drinking about a third of the bottle and washing down the noodles, the male student wore a look of relief. Ayaka helped clean his mouth. His mouth must have been covered in sauce because he was eating yakisoba, and the wet wipe she used was stained brown.

As she dabbed at his mouth, the boy scowled and grumbled, "Could you not treat me like a little kid?"

Ayaka wiped his mouth again, grinning as she did. Amane reasoned that even though he seemed a little annoyed by it, the fact that he didn't try to stop her showed that they had a strong relationship.

"Um, is this your boyfriend, Kido?"

"Oh, bingo! This is my childhood friend and boyfriend. Go on, Sou sweetie, introduce yourself."

"Do you think I'm the kind of person who won't do it unless you prod me like a kid…?"

"It's just because you're shy, sweetie. Go on, he's not a bad person."

"If he was a bad person, you wouldn't be introducing us in the first place… I'm Souji Kayano."

When Souji nodded in greeting, Ayaka patted his head as if to congratulate him on a job well done, and he brushed her hand away.

Ayaka didn't seem to mind, as if she was used to it. Feeling impressed in a certain sense by how strong Ayaka's resolve must be, Amane looked Souji over.

The only information he had heard from Ayaka was that the boy had amazing muscles, so he'd expected her boyfriend's nice physique to be more apparent, but... Amane could tell that he was taller, but he couldn't quite get a sense for his build through his school uniform. If anything, Amane thought that Kazuya had a nicer build.

He tried to check him out inconspicuously so he wouldn't appear rude, but Ayaka seemed to be able to tell what Amane was looking at, and smiled very playfully.

"Sou here is the type that looks great when he takes it all off, okay?"

"W-when he takes it all off..."

"That's right, Miss Shiina, my boyfriend is really impressive. Oh-ho-ho!" Ayaka said, wearing a subtly smirking smile.

Seeing her grin, Amane was thinking it would probably be best not to let Mahiru hear too much more about the subject. But it was Souji himself who objected.

"Knock it off, stop bragging. It's embarrassing... Actually, wait, what are you telling people when I'm not around? Have you been bragging about my muscles again?"

"I've just been saying that my boyfriend has great muscles."

"I wish you would stop that... They're not even anything to boast about."

"How can you say that?! To me, they're the best in the world!"

"She says, when she was drooling over a bodybuilding special on TV the other day..."

"Ah, that's just like a little snack I have sometimes... Your muscles are staples *and* a luxury I can't live without! You're special, Sou!" Ayaka declared plainly, with great seriousness.

Amane was too focused on the part about bodybuilders to notice her going on about her boyfriend.

Does she really like muscles that much...? I don't understand her world.

If anything, Mahiru had a thing for certain smells, so in a sense he couldn't help feeling like she might get along well with Ayaka. He had complicated feelings about hearing them talk about what parts of their boyfriends' bodies they fetishized, so if possible, he would have preferred them to talk about it in private, someplace where the boys themselves were not.

When Amane took a step back and looked at Ayaka, amazed in several senses of the word, Souji seemed to more or less pick up on what he was thinking, and without trying to hide his exasperation, he whacked Ayaka gently on the head.

"That's enough. You're scaring him off."

"That's because you're saying weird stuff, Sou sweetie."

"...Sorry, man, my girl Ayaka is, well—"

"What's wrong with me?!"

She gave her boyfriend a sour look, but it seemed to be just more of their teasing.

Even as she stuck her lip out in a pout as if she was mad at him, Ayaka was casually, lovingly stroking his muscles. Amane couldn't help but smile.

Souji didn't seem to mind, or rather, he let her do as she pleased, probably because she always did that. As he let it happen, he bobbed his head in a little bow at Amane, and without thinking, Amane also let his head bob a few times.

As for Mahiru, she had been keeping silent, as if she was thinking something over, but for some reason she suddenly clung to Amane and started patting his stomach.

"...You know, Amane looks great when he takes it off, too."

"It doesn't have to be a competition, and I don't look that great. If I had to guess, I'd have a hard time measuring up to him."

"You look plenty good to me."

She was touching Amane and blushing as she did, so a bitter smile rose to his face of its own accord as he wondered why she was doing that.

"Come to think of it, have you two eaten lunch yet, Fujimiya?"

As he was calming Mahiru down, suddenly Ayaka asked the question like it had just occurred to her.

They'd been on the same shift, so they had rotated out at the same time. But Ayaka's boyfriend had been waiting for her, so she'd wasted no time switching out. Their other classmates on the same shift probably hadn't gotten their food as quickly as she had.

"No, we're about to. We were thinking of going to buy some *yakisoba* or something."

"Ah, *yakisoba*? It's real good, Sou's class is the one making it." Ayaka laughed and added, "Sou ate most of it though, huh?"

"That's because you kept telling me to eat more. You were basically forcing it on me," Souji shot back quietly.

"I see, okay so you two want to get some yakisoba, right? In that case, I'll give you this."

She held out some kind of ticket to Mahiru with a smile. It was good for one hundred yen off an order of yakisoba.

"It's a discount coupon for friends and family. Sweetie said that I can give them to other folks I'm friends with… They're good, right?"

"If you want to give one to them, I think you can. My class still gets a sale either way."

"Whoo-hoo!"

Ayaka grinned and thrust two tickets at them. Amane looked her in the face, feeling grateful and a little guilty, and Ayaka broke into a carefree grin again.

"Ah, you don't have to worry about it, you know? I'm sure we'll get sick of eating so much yakisoba, so we won't use them. Besides, if I had to say, I feel more like a hot dog right now anyway."

Ayaka laughed and added that she wanted protein more than carbs. Amane thought that a hot dog seemed like it had a lot of fat, too, but he decided to not point that out. He meekly said, "Thanks," and decided to accept the favor with gratitude.

"Thank you very much, Miss Kido. Allow me to return the favor someday."

"Oh, go on! I wasn't looking for any kind of reward...ah, but then, Miss Shiina?"

"Y-yes?"

"How good are Fujimiya's muscles?"

Mahiru's expression was timid, and a shade of astonishment appeared on her face as she marveled at Ayaka's question. Mahiru blinked repeatedly in surprise, then got flustered for some reason.

"I'm n-not telling, Amane is mine."

"Oh, how cute. No, no, my sweet Sou is the best in the world, okay? I'm simply curious, that's all."

"Looking at other guys, are you?"

"N-no I would never! Believe me, Sou sweetie!"

Picking up on Mahiru's panic, Ayaka waved her hand in front of her face, but she seemed to know that Souji was half joking. She puffed her cheeks out and grumbled that Souji was being a jerk in a voice that had a slightly sweet ring to it. Then she turned to Mahiru, who was still a little bit on her guard, with a beaming smile.

"Sou's got the wrong idea. But if he's got the right stuff to start with...I mean, I'd like to help him develop...don't you think it's a waste? Fujimiya's got the height and he's slender. He'd look really nice if he put on some more muscle."

"...If he gets any better looking than he already is, I'll be in trouble."

"Ah, Fujimiya's the real deal after today, though. His popularity is gonna go through the roof!"

Ayaka nodded with a know-it-all look on her face, while Mahiru stuck her lip out in a pout.

Amane wasn't sure whether he should be glad that Mahiru was being frank with Ayaka, or whether he should poke fun at her for starting to get jealous.

He knew that he wasn't likely to get popular enough that Mahiru would have to worry. To begin with, if he had been attractive enough for Ayaka to approach him, she would have had plenty of chances to do so already. Of course, it never would have worked.

Anyway, there were plenty of people more handsome than Amane, and he was not as developed as a person as Mahiru thought.

Even so, Mahiru seemed concerned. With a gentle, wry smile, Amane ruffled her hair.

"I really have no interest in any one other than you, Mahiru, and even if someone did like me, I would never return the feelings of someone who forced their way between a happy couple, so please, don't worry."

"Even if that's true, I don't like the idea."

"Well, I feel pretty much the same way, yeah? Come on, you don't have to worry like that, it's all right."

"...I feel like you're not understanding me..."

He tried to set her at ease, but for some reason, Mahiru frowned again in apparent dissatisfaction, leaving him confused.

Ayaka laughed and teased, "It's hard out there, even for Miss Shiina."

After Amane and Mahiru had gratefully accepted the discount tickets from Ayaka and Souji, the couples parted ways. Amane and Mahiru quickly purchased some yakisoba, and went to the back garden to eat.

There were no open seats in the established lounge areas, and they couldn't very well linger in the dressing rooms where all the equipment had been stashed, so by process of elimination, they went to the back garden, which seemed likely to be open.

Outsiders weren't allowed all the way into the back garden, so there were only a few students there. There were plenty of places to sit.

Amane spread a towel over the bench where Mahiru wanted to sit, and they took a seat in a spot that was under the shade of a tree. Then he leaned against the backrest lavishly.

"You know, when things are too lively, I just start to lose it."

"Heh-heh, you do prefer a quiet environment, don't you, Amane?"

"And I don't like people looking you up and down, either. Actually, I hate it."

"It's not that big of a deal, though…"

"It wears away at my soul."

There had been no way out of it, so he had endured it all day, but he hadn't enjoyed it. Since Mahiru had changed into her school uniform, the stares had settled down, more so than when she was dressed as a maid, but she was still beautiful and continued to attract a lot of attention.

Well, Mahiru seemed to have resigned herself to it and grown accustomed to the attention, so he couldn't raise too many objections and just grumbled his complaints quietly.

Mahiru also seemed to understand, because she smiled wryly, as if she was not sure what to do, and patted his head to comfort him.

Amane sighed softly as he accepted the gesture. "I bet even more people will come in tomorrow with how popular we were, and because we're working in the afternoon."

"Well, if we can make it through tomorrow, it'll be over then… Come to think of it, what about your parents?"

Mahiru seemed to think it was strange that they hadn't seen Amane's parents, since they had been eager to come see the two teenagers in their costumes.

Amane scratched his cheek and shrugged. "They said they're coming tomorrow. And that they've got some vacation time, so they're getting a hotel and should be here for a couple of days."

"Oh, really?!"

"Why do you look so happy about it?"

"Because recently, I got your father to promise to teach me his mom's home cooking techniques, and my chance is coming sooner than I thought."

"He's a man, but he calls it 'Mom's home cooking'...well, I guess if I had to say, I'm more familiar with the taste of my dad's cooking anyway."

Amane's parents, Shihoko and Shuuto, each did their share of cooking dinner on their allotted days, so Amane was very familiar with the way they both made food. However, his mother Shihoko's cooking for her otherwise all-male household focused on bold flavors, high volume, and many options, so although it certainly was his mother's cooking, it didn't really have a 'Mom's home cooking' feel to it.

His father Shuuto was better at cooking, and his flavors were more delicate but comforting. The taste of home for Amane had to be his father's cooking.

He wasn't skilled enough that Mahiru needed to learn from him...but it sounded like it was important to her to learn the flavors of the Fujimiya household, and for some reason, she seemed determined to do so.

"I'm really quite satisfied with your cooking, you know?"

"That's one thing, this is another. I want to be able to make things for you whenever you feel like eating them."

"Got it... But to me, the flavor of your cooking is the flavor of home, so you don't have to force yourself to learn."

"…The second I let my guard down, you go and say stuff like that."

Sooner or later, she would have him by the stomach—actually, it was fair to say that she already did. He got to eat delicious food every day, so there was no doubt that the taste of Mahiru's cooking was the taste of home. It was the flavor of their time together, distinct from the tastes of the Fujimiya household.

Out-of-season cherry blossoms bloomed on Mahiru's cheeks and he could tell by the way she slapped him with the wet wipe she was holding that she was quietly trying to get him to turn the same color.

The yakisoba sitting on her lap seemed in danger of falling off. As he moved it out of the way, he ruffled her hair in an attempt to pacify her.

The gesture lifted her hair, which fell in loose waves thanks to the braids she had been wearing that morning. The increased volume seemed to reach Mahiru's cheeks, which she puffed up in displeasure.

"…Amane, you don't think that you can get away with that just by patting my head, do you?"

"I don't think that, but I do think you like it."

"Goes to show how hopeless you are."

Mahiru huffed and pretended to be curt with him, but Amane could see the redness of her cheeks, and he chuckled quietly at the spoiled Mahiru, and this time stroked her head and put her hair back in order.

Amane and Mahiru finished their lunch and resumed their tour of the school. But everywhere they went, they faced stares and whispers, and Mahiru looked like she was getting a little tired.

It was possible that they were attracting extra attention because they were holding hands so that they didn't lose each other, but the one thing that Mahiru seemed most reluctant to do was to let go of Amane's hand. Mahiru's fingers, entwined unassumingly but firmly with Amane's, insisted that he couldn't let her go.

He got looks of encouragement from classmates who had been with them in the first year of school, when the two of them had their first chance meeting. When he looked at Mahiru, she softly leaned in close to him, wearing a graceful smile, so he knew she had no intention of letting go. If anything, she seemed even more insistent on holding on.

...Not that I really mind, but I think the whole school knows that we're dating now.

Pretty much every student at their school knew when Mahiru had first started going out with Amane. She had boldly announced at the school sports day that Amane was her important person, then declared that they had started dating at the beginning of the following week.

Since Mahiru was famous not only among their year, but also with students in the upper and lower grades, the news spread quickly. The disappointment among the boys had been terrible. Amane had even been hounded for answers by an unfamiliar upperclassman once, when Mahiru wasn't around.

According to reports from their classmates, after that incident, Mahiru had rushed to put a stop to it all with a smile on her face.

They had overcome such obstacles and continued dating, so at this point it was safe to assume that nobody else was going to try to get in between the couple. They didn't have to make a big deal about it, just walking around together was enough.

But Mahiru wouldn't leave Amane's side. It was like she was expecting something to happen. Even after they left their classmates behind, Mahiru stayed snuggled up to him pretty closely.

"Something the matter?"

"You look really sharp today."

"What are you talking about?"

"Well, your hairstyle, and, like, your whole attitude."

"I mean, I did come out with my hair still styled from our café."

"So that's why."

"I don't really understand, but…"

If it was possible for Amane to become more popular by changing his hairstyle, he would have already been popular before he even started officially going out with Mahiru, so he didn't think he was so popular that she needed to cling to him and assert her claim. Personally, he was happy to have her clinging to him, but on the other hand, having her so close meant that he couldn't help but notice the feeling of her body, so he found himself wishing that she would pull away just a little bit more.

Mahiru herself seemed to enjoy it, so he was letting her do as she pleased, but he couldn't help but feel a little bit uncomfortable.

Amane thought about how, thanks to Mahiru, he had even gotten used to being the center of attention. As he walked slowly around the school with her, he tried as hard as he could to ignore the crowds around them.

Amane looked at the pamphlet that had been given out listing all the different exhibitions, but Mahiru was already quietly leading the way—actually, she was steering them directly toward the haunted house.

…I get the sense that Mahiru doesn't really go for scary stuff, though.

The one time they had watched some horror together, Mahiru had put on a brave front, but she had gone very pale and had gripped his hand very tightly. Her words and the expression on her face had been at odds, and Amane had figured that she probably didn't care for the horror genre.

But maybe she had decided that it wouldn't be a problem, since of course a haunted house constructed on a student budget couldn't possibly compare with a properly built television set.

"Do you want to go to the haunted house that badly?"

"Eh?"

Mahiru stopped suddenly and looked timidly up at him. Her expression looked decidedly lost. Maybe she had been meaning to walk around aimlessly, and hadn't thought that far ahead.

Mahiru looked around, wearing a stiff expression, like a machine in need of oil. Amane was certain that she had not even considered going to the haunted house.

"Th-that wasn't my intention, but…"

"This whole time I was sure that was where you were leading us. Although, you can't really handle scary things, so I guess that was ridiculous."

"…That's not true."

"Look at me and say that again. You can't even look me in the eye."

Mahiru tried to evade the issue rather than admit to her weakness, but her expression and her posture were ruining her chances. Amane was not gracious enough to believe her, in spite of how obviously flustered she was.

I don't think being sensitive to scary things is really anything to be ashamed of, though.

Rather, he thought it was cute. But Mahiru herself seemed unhappy.

He had been thinking how charming it was, but Mahiru seemed to have figured that out, and she looked up at Amane with a little bit of dissatisfaction in her eyes. But those eyes were watery, maybe because she hadn't gotten over the shock of the earlier incident, so it probably didn't have the impact she was hoping for.

"Really, it's fine. We'll go to the haunted house, too."

©Hanekoto

"It's fine, huh? All right, how about we watch a horror movie together soon?"

"…Th-that would be great."

"Your voice is really shaky, isn't it?"

He'd said it more or less as a joke, but Mahiru was posturing and agreeing to go, which conversely put Amane in a tough spot.

"Are you gonna be all right, putting on a brave front? Don't come crying to me when you can't sleep alone."

"I'm not bluffing. And if the worst happens…I'll make you take responsibility."

"Living people can be scarier than ghosts, you know."

"I don't think you're scary, Amane, and besides, we've already slept together several times, so there."

She pressed herself tightly against his arm and turned her eyes upward at him. Quickly, he pressed a finger over Mahiru's mouth, and softly let out a sigh.

Sure, he had dozed off in her presence even before they'd started dating, and Mahiru had even stayed over at his place, plus they had slept in the same bed at his parents' house over the summer break. In a certain sense, she had spent the night multiple times.

However, it was a statement that seemed extremely likely to invite misunderstanding. The students around them were already murmuring faintly. They didn't actually have that kind of relationship yet, and Amane had complicated feelings about being misunderstood.

"…That sounds like an invitation to me."

"Stop getting the wrong idea. Anyway, you're the one who invited me to stay over, Amane."

"I didn't have any ulterior motives. I just wanted to see you shiver."

"I'd call that an ulterior motive."

She slapped him lightly on his side, so he grasped her prodding hand again and stopped her.

Mahiru seemed happy to have her hand grasped, because her face, which had been looking a little dissatisfied, softened into a smile. So Amane smiled back at Mahiru and pulled her by the hand.

Of course, he pulled her in the direction of the haunted house.

"…Um?"

"I thought we'd go in, since we came all the way here. You're the one who first said we would go through the haunted house, after all."

"I—I certainly did say that. B-but you d-don't have to b-be mean…"

Mahiru squirmed restlessly and looked up at him with faintly misty eyes. Amane chuckled a little and mercilessly pulled her toward the haunted house.

After that, she clung tightly to him the whole time they were inside the haunted house, but for the sake of her reputation, he decided not to mention it to Chitose and the others.

After they got out of the haunted house, Mahiru seemed somewhat exhausted from surprise and fright. Supporting her from behind, Amane headed for a lounge area, but he suddenly caught sight of the back of a familiar figure, and an unintended gasp escaped his lips.

"…Is that Itsuki's…?"

It wasn't someone he saw very often, so he called out timidly toward the person, and they turned around, their back straight as a rod.

It was a man the same age as Amane's parents, Shihoko and Shuuto. Despite having a handsome face, he was wearing a craggy expression with no trace of softness or gentleness.

When he saw the man's face, exactly as it appeared in his memories, Amane breathed a sigh of relief that he was not mistaken and formally straightened his posture. Beside him, Mahiru looked up at him questioningly, so he whispered to her, quietly, so that the man couldn't hear him, "It's Itsuki's dad."

"Nice to see you again. I've changed my hair a little, so it might be hard to recognize me, but I'm Fujimiya."

The man who was Itsuki's father, Daiki, took a good look at Amane's face, and his expression, that people said looked unapproachable, seemed to soften a bit.

"Fujimiya, huh? I hardly recognize you."

"Ah-ha-ha, well, that must be because I used to look so gloomy."

"That's not what I meant, but...I was thinking you look like you've gained some confidence, which is great. No need to put yourself down."

Itsuki had often complained that his father scolded him a lot, but Daiki seemed to like Amane a fair bit and appeared to be impressed by the changes he saw.

Amane had to admit that Daiki could be hardheaded when it came to his son Itsuki, but for the most part he was reasonable and sensible, so it was no hardship for Amane to speak with him. If he had to say one way or another, he found it rather enjoyable.

Daiki sounded and looked impressed, which made Amane feel a little embarrassed. Then Daiki's gaze shifted to Mahiru.

"Who's that young lady?"

"Ah, umm. This is the girl I'm dating."

It was an unusually reserved way of introducing her. He'd chosen it because he wasn't sure how friendly he should be with Daiki. It was quite difficult to know how to act toward a friend's parents, so there was no helping feeling that way.

He could tell by the way she had stiffened slightly that Mahiru was feeling embarrassed and awkward, but she put on her angelic smile, and bowed her head slightly.

To Mahiru, this man was a stranger, so she treated him as such. Given Daiki's personality, that was probably the right choice anyway.

"How do you do? I'm Mahiru Shiina. As Amane was kind enough to explain, the two of us are dating."

"It's very nice to meet you. I am Itsuki's father, Daiki Akazawa."

Daiki bowed politely at the waist, then glanced over at Amane. Amane got the feeling that Daiki was trying to tell him he was a pretty smooth operator, but he purposely pretended not to notice and smiled cheerfully back at him.

"I see…well, what can I say? So Fujimiya is dating a girl, huh? I hadn't heard anything about it, what a surprise!"

"Not a word from Itsuki?"

"He basically doesn't talk to me, you know. I'm sure he just thought there was no need to tell me."

"Well, I don't think his friend's dating situation is something he'd go out of his way to talk about anyway."

Though Amane felt disappointed to hear that Itsuki's relationship with his father was strained as always, he didn't let it show outwardly.

"So you're dating Fujimiya…which must mean you've been looking after my fool of a son, too. I'm sorry for all the trouble."

"Not at all, in fact, we're very indebted to Mister Akazawa."

"Are you sure he isn't making a nuisance of himself?"

"Far from it. He's kind and thoughtful and helps us out all the time. I sincerely hope to be good friends with Mister Akazawa for a long time to come."

After hearing Mahiru praise his son without making any jokes about how nosy he could be, Daiki sighed with admiration.

"…Fujimiya, seems like you've found a wonderful girl. I'm happy to see it."

"I sure have. Mahiru is a fine young lady."

"P-please don't make jokes like that right now."

She'd probably never imagined that Amane would commend her

like that out loud in front of his friend's father, and it was easy to see the color rise in her pale cheeks.

She cast her eyes down bashfully, and casually launched a direct attack against his back with her palm in such a way that Daiki wouldn't notice, which made Amane chuckle quietly. Her attack only had the force of a light slap, so it didn't hurt or even tickle. Instead, it made the corners of his mouth curl up in amusement.

"It looks like you get along well, which is the most important thing, although it seems like you might get in trouble for that kind of behavior. I'm happy to see it, though."

"Sorry, we'll be careful. By the way, have you visited our classroom today?"

"No, I was intending to, but…how do I put this? There was something about the atmosphere in there…it was hard for me to go in."

"Ah…"

Daiki was the kind of person who didn't have much interest in these sorts of exhibitions. He was also the type who had never expressed any interest in pop culture like manga or video games. Considering all that, it wasn't strange that he found it difficult to walk into their classroom.

"I'm sure it would put the students in an awkward position if I were to go in alone. Especially with the way I look."

"In your case, sir, I think it has more to do with the expression on your face than your appearance. If you'd like, we could go in with you? It's our class, but I did want to go visit as a customer."

"No, I couldn't possibly impose on you like that. Not when you're spending your precious free time together with your sweetheart. Besides…I'm sure that girl must be in the classroom as well."

"…Yes, she is."

"I hate the idea of her seeing me and it causing her shrink back, or feel uneasy. If we come face-to-face, I'll probably lash out at her, you see," Daiki said with an uncomfortable smile.

Amane frowned, but didn't question him any further.

Amane didn't have very good feelings about the relationship between Chitose and Daiki. However, he knew that Chitose didn't hold any malice toward Daiki. And that Daiki had his own way of thinking which made him reject Chitose.

Even though he understood that, Amane was Itsuki's friend, and he wished that they would settle the issues between them.

"Sorry for bothering you kids. I'll walk around to the other rooms."

"But..."

"I wouldn't want to ruin the mood. You two have fun," Daiki said, and walked away before Amane and Mahiru could even try to stop him.

Amane let out a soft sigh.

"...He's still on bad terms with Chitose?"

"Yeah... That's kind of a whole thing, but Itsuki's dad isn't a bad person. There are some folks he just can't get along with. I think Daiki's personality is inherently a bad match for people like Itsuki and Chitose."

Fundamentally, Daiki had a deeply serious and stubborn nature, something that even Amane, who had only interacted with him a little bit, could tell.

In contrast, he wouldn't exactly say that people like Itsuki and Chitose were foolish, but they certainly didn't follow the standard straight and narrow path in life, and they were unconventional and flexible people.

Amane didn't think that the two of them, who would never want to force themselves to fit a certain mold just because someone else told them to, were likely to obediently listen to what Daiki said, so it made sense that they didn't get along.

But if someone asked Amane if he blamed Daiki for it, he would say that he did not. Though many of Daiki's demands were old-fashioned, they were well within the realm of common sense.

"Itsuki's dad has some expectations that are a little too strict, for sure. It's not that he just treats Chitose harshly out of spite... And that's exactly why they're stuck with no way to resolve their issues."

If Daiki was going to approve of Chitose, he surely would have done so already.

Amane knew that it couldn't feel very good to have one of your parents butting into your love life, but he could also understand why a parent would want their child to find the best partner they could.

Itsuki almost never talked about it, and Amane wasn't usually aware of what was going on in his home life, but the Akazawa family had high social standing, which probably compounded the issue.

"You'd think it would be better for them if she could do something and gain his approval, but... It may be impossible."

"Right, maybe... I think the two of them go really well together, and that they are deeply connected. It seems wrong to me to try to separate them... I wish he would give it up."

"You're right about that... And I think Itsuki's dad knows it, too, and that he's interfering as little as possible now. But until one of them folds and they come to an agreement, things will probably stay awkward."

After sighing once more, Mahiru also frowned, looking troubled, and rested her head against Amane's shoulder. "But I wish there was something we could do," she mumbled quietly.

After parting with Daiki, Amane and Mahiru headed toward their own classroom, thinking they could buy some refreshments and take a break at the same time. Compared to the other classrooms, quite a line had formed at the reception desk.

They had peeked outside occasionally, even while they were on their own shift, but now they could see that the place had been booming since morning. It looked like their initial popularity had only attracted more visitors.

Even though it was their own classroom, customers were customers, and Amane obediently lined up with Mahiru to wait their turn. Their classmates looked busy, running their eyes down a list of names.

"Oh, Fujimiya and the an—and Miss Shiina. Don't tell me you've come back to help?"

"Unfortunately, you've got the wrong idea. We thought we'd give the customer side of things a try. And also see how Itsuki and Chitose are doing."

"Ah, those two are getting along great. Well, kinda."

"What's that supposed to mean?"

"No matter what we do, Itsuki's waaay too flashy."

"That's because being flashy is basically part of his identity."

"Rude."

Itsuki was always cheerful and funny, and he would probably never completely lose that unless something really extreme happened. For an exhibition like this one, although he was taking it seriously, his usual attitude was going to show through. He wasn't likely to leave his joking behind.

And there were some students who appreciated Itsuki's humor, which made him a popular butler in his own way. Anyway, since it was a student exhibition, he didn't have to adhere too strictly to butler etiquette, and he could get away with merely looking the part.

"Okay, so I can put you down as a party of two, right? You'll probably have to wait a little while, though."

"It's crowded, so that makes sense... Are you doing okay, Mahiru? You're not too tired?"

"I'm fine. I—I am tired, but mentally, after that, um, earlier program..."

"That's because you pretended to be tough and went in."

"...I wasn't pretending."

Mahiru averted her eyes. Seeing her bluff like that only made him want to tease her more, but if he teased her too much, she would pout, so he decided to avoid mentioning it again.

Instead, he whispered quietly, "Remember your promise about the horror movie." She glared at him with a tremor in her eyes, but this time, Amane was the one who pretended not to notice.

The boy at the reception desk, who had been watching from the sidelines, also glared at Amane. "Do that somewhere else, please."

Feeling uncomfortable, Amane looked elsewhere.

They waited outside, and when their turn came, they followed the host into their own classroom, where they were greeted by two familiar faces. Amane felt himself frown.

Sure enough, Itsuki and Chitose were their servers, just as he had told the receptionist he wanted.

They were wearing more formal smiles than they had during the practice periods, and in response to Amane's faintly displeased expression, he saw their cheeks start twitching.

They were looking at him like they had succeeded in playing some sort of prank, which nearly set Amane's face twitching in exasperation.

"Welcome back, Master. And the missus!"

"Hey, come on, Itsuki! That greeting's not in the manual!"

Basically, since they were supposed to be running a maid and butler style of café, the class had settled on a unified way to address

©Hanekoto

their customers. But when his two friends purposely addressed them in a totally wrong way, Amane couldn't hold out any longer, and his face screwed up into an exasperated grimace.

Mahiru averted her eyes bashfully. She was probably embarrassed by being called "the missus."

"No, no, preposterous! This greeting is listed in a special page of the manual that's only for the two of you—a page I kept top secret."

"You're sure you're not making that up?"

"Now, now. Allow us to show you to your seats."

It wasn't good to give them special treatment in front of the other customers, but in spite of the reproachful glances, Itsuki showed no concern at all.

It seemed like it would be pointless to say anything, so Amane reluctantly followed their prompting to his seat.

Amane briefly had his attention captured by the elegance of Mahiru's movements as she smoothly took her seat in the chair that Itsuki pulled out for her.

With a grin, Chitose said, "Did you enjoy your break?" Following the manual, she presented them with menus that were actually entirely unnecessary, since Amane had completely memorized the offerings.

"Mm, yes, we did enjoy it. We haven't finished going around to every room yet, so we plan to keep going after this."

"That's great, just great. I figured sweet Mahiru must have been looking forward to her break, since she kept hoping it would come sooner."

"Was I really that bad?"

"Well you know, she told me she wanted to walk around and see all the different spots."

He glanced over at Mahiru, who was changing the subject by ordering. "One A set, please," she requested, with faintly red cheeks.

At home, he hadn't really seen her get excited about the culture festival, but it sounded like, in her own way, Mahiru had been looking forward to spending the time with Amane.

He smiled a little at the charming Mahiru, and, as he promised himself he would ask her for the details later, he ordered the same thing as her. Perhaps she could tell what he was thinking, because she glared at him just a little bit, but she didn't seem unhappy about it, so that gave him some peace of mind.

Chitose took his order and didn't even try to hide her grin as she went to tell the back of the house their orders. As she left, Amane remembered the sack of donuts he had in his lap and held them out to Itsuki.

The donuts were round, bite-size, deep-fried balls of dough, so he would be able to snack on them when he had free time. Amane recalled that there should be toothpicks set out in the back, in which case, it would be easy for the other staff to eat them as well, without getting their hands dirty.

"Oh, that's right. Another class is selling these, so I brought some for everyone. Give some to the guys in the back, too, whenever they have a break."

"Oh, awesome, thanks!"

"It's fine, it was my idea, so you don't have to worry about it, but if you're going to thank me, do it more like a butler…"

"Oh, Master, your favor is truly a gift to us all…"

"Yeah, never mind. You can drop that, too."

Itsuki was wearing a happy face. He muttered to himself that he'd eaten lunch but was already getting hungry again.

Amane smiled at him and felt guilty that he was about to say something that threatened to dampen his friend's mood a little bit.

"Hey, Itsuki?"

"Hmm?"

"I ran into your dad. I thought you should know."

Amane could see Itsuki's body stiffen a little.

He'd tried to do his best to report it when Chitose wasn't around, so that's why he had chosen that moment. But it looked like the revelation was already sapping Itsuki's motivation to serve the customers, so Amane honestly wished he hadn't said anything.

Itsuki's usually unshakable, easygoing smile dimmed, and in its place, a sour expression rose to his face. Then in an effort to conceal it, he forced himself to form a smile again.

"Ah, he didn't ask about Chitose or anything," Amane added. "He said it was hard to come in here, so he went off somewhere else. That's all I wanted to report."

"Ah... Well, my dad doesn't handle stuff like this very well. Even if you get him to come, I mean, Chi will probably get upset about it, so it's probably for the best that he doesn't come in, but..."

Itsuki shrugged and grumbled. "Even though I gave him a ticket out of obligation, I never actually expected him to come, you know. If he comes back again, I'll ask him. At any rate, I don't think he's coming to see me today."

With a smile that made it hard to read what he was thinking, Itsuki returned to the back of the café carrying the bag of donuts in one hand. Amane sighed softly.

...I really hope things go well, somehow.

He assumed that their issues couldn't be resolved so simply. But going slowly was okay, and all he could do was hope that they could find a way to understand each other.

Chitose carried out their orders instead of Itsuki, and cocked her head curiously when she saw the expressions that Amane and Mahiru were wearing. They were both feeling a little down because of the thing with Daiki.

"Oh, what's up, you two? Have a fight?"

"Do you really think we would fight?"

"Normally, I'd say that all couples have arguments, but...in your case, you both listen to each other, so amazingly I'm not sure I can dispute you on that one, Amane."

She answered him in a low, earnest voice that blended exasperation with admiration. But as far as Amane was concerned, he didn't think it was all that unusual.

Fundamentally, Mahiru was gentle and open-minded, so she almost never got angry anyway. Moreover, she seldom got upset with him. Even if she was mad because of someone else, it wasn't really in her nature for her to lose her temper.

If he got into an argument with a girl like that, it was basically guaranteed to be Amane's fault, and if it came to that, they were more likely to start a discussion than have it out in an argument. He would want to know what had gone wrong and how he had hurt her feelings, and the two of them would talk about the reasons and solutions.

He had never made her so mad that they couldn't even talk about it, and if it ever happened, he would be sure to apologize profusely.

So they almost never found themselves quarreling.

Mahiru also heard the word *fight*, and repeatedly blinked her caramel-colored eyes in surprise, as if to say that she had never actually experienced that. Amane smiled a little because that was just the reaction he'd expected.

She had never really been angry at Amane. He could recall one time she told him off when she thought he was being spineless, but that wasn't true anger. More like a scolding, and if anything, she had actually been angry on Amane's behalf.

"Well, suffice it to say that we're not fighting. We've just got a lot of difficult things on our minds and are worrying over what to do about them."

"Hmm? Well, so long as you two aren't fighting, then I'm happy. But in other news, Amane, aren't your parents coming?"

The word *parents* made his body stiffen for a moment, but Chitose didn't seem to notice and leaned in close.

Amane felt a little relieved that she seemed to have pushed Daiki's presence to the back of her mind for the moment.

"Well, according to my dear Mahiru, I'm going to get along great with your mother, so I'm curious to meet her. I've just got to say hello."

"Not only do you seem like you'll get along great, she's basically your kindred spirit, and I can just see how Mahiru is going to suffer as a result."

It didn't just seem like Chitose would get along with his mother, Shihoko. Their ways of thinking were quite similar as well. Amane thought back nostalgically to when he had first met Chitose, and he recalled how she had been just as exhausting as his mother.

They were exactly alike in their love for cute things, their extreme touchy-feeliness, and their intense love for Mahiru, so Mahiru would probably get doted on and played with by both of them.

Mahiru seemed to have no trouble imagining the scene. The corners of her mouth twitched and trembled, but Amane pretended not to see it.

Well, you're either going to be turned into a dress-up doll, or have them hanging all over you, so best of luck.

None of that would hurt her, so he didn't have to worry about that. Mahiru was giving him a pleading look, but there was nothing that Amane could do to save her from her fate. He hoped she had the strong will to endure it.

"Well, go easy on her, okay? Also, shouldn't you be getting back to work?"

"Eep, you're right, Mako is glaring at me!"

Makoto, who was on the same shift, was staring at Chitose like he had some choice words for her. As Amane suspected, she wasn't supposed to be casually chatting.

Chitose stuck out her tongue in a playful bid for forgiveness, and Makoto gave her a chilly look, so Amane urged her to hurry up and get back to work.

Watching Chitose's back as she reluctantly left to return to work, Amane exhaled softly.

"All I can do is cheer you on from the sidelines, but good luck, Mahiru."

"You're not getting involved?"

"No, there's nothing I can do about those two, not when they're all fired up like that. Do your best. If you really hate the idea, then you have to be clear."

"H-hate it, huh…? Um…I'm definitely going to end up being their dress-up doll, aren't I?"

"Probably, yeah."

Even under normal circumstances, Amane's mother liked to dote on Mahiru and dress her up, so once she met Chitose, she was likely to start scheming even more energetically. After all, his mother already considered Mahiru to be her daughter-in-law, so she seemed likely to drag her to a boutique and make her try on this and that, and then buy her several outfits. He could imagine Chitose accompanying them with enthusiasm.

But when it came to all that, Amane didn't have much power to stop them. His mother had always wanted a daughter, and she had taken such a liking to Mahiru specifically.

"Well, if it means you're going to get all dressed up, then from where I stand, I don't think there's any need for me to stop it."

"When you put it that way, you know I can't refuse…"

"I mean, if you want to turn down the two of them and let me dress you up as I please instead, that would be okay, too."

He didn't exactly have anything in particular that he wanted to make her wear, but there was something intriguing about the idea of getting Mahiru to put on clothes that he thought would look good on her.

"…I'd like you to do that, even if the two of them weren't involved. If it means dressing me the way you like, then yes, please," Mahiru mumbled quietly and averted her eyes bashfully.

Mahiru was what he liked, and that was true no matter what she was wearing, but he couldn't say that there, so he just smiled happily over how charming his girlfriend was as he slowly sipped his coffee.

Amane drank his coffee as he waited for her to calm down a little. As he looked around, he keenly realized just how effective the rumors had been in drawing customers.

They had thought that they had set up quite a lot of tables, but Amane still didn't see a single open seat. It had been the same while Mahiru and him were on their shift. They constantly had a full house, with no break in the customer traffic.

There was no need to exaggerate—Yuuta and Mahiru may have been the main attractions, but even after the two of them had finished their shifts, customers were still thronging to the café, probably thanks to the fancy costumes.

Apparently, seeing young people who usually wore school uniforms all dressed up in maid and butler costumes struck a chord with people.

For Amane's part, he merely thought that it all looked very out of place.

Chitose, for example, was a person who Amane had never imagined would wear a uniform for serving other people.

He glanced over at Chitose, who was attending to a customer while lavishing them with a cheerful smile, but he didn't see any of the industriousness that her uniform would lead him to imagine. However, her friendly, animated disposition certainly matched her short maid outfit, he couldn't argue with that.

"…What's going on with Chitose?"

While he was watching Chitose, thinking that she had way too much energy, Mahiru spoke up in a curious voice. She seemed to have somehow managed to shut away her bashfulness.

"Mm, well…I didn't really get this feeling when we were working together, but maybe our classmates feel uncomfortable in these kinds of costumes. It's not like we're used to wearing this stuff."

"Heh-heh, that's because clothes like these aren't things that we would ever normally wear."

"The novelty of it has to be one of the reasons why the customers are coming in. Plus, the customers are saying we look cute and cool. Well, it's definitely true the outfits do look great on everyone."

There were some guests mixed in among the students sitting in the customer seats, but most customers seemed to be there to see a particular employee. Amane could hear voices evaluating who among the servers looked especially cute or cool.

He wasn't unsympathetic to their feelings, but since they were loud enough to be heard, the servers were having to force themselves to smile.

After reviewing the employees' difficult situation, Amane looked at Mahiru and saw that she was wearing a concerned expression with a faint bit of tension in her brow.

"What's the matter?"

"Nothing… Amane, do you also…think everyone…or actually, do think that the girls…look cute?"

"Yeah, about as much as I normally do."

He somehow or other sensed what Mahiru was trying to say, so he smiled, barely trying to hide his lips with the knuckle of his bent finger.

"If I'm being objective, I'd say that they're undeniably cute and charming. But you're the only one I love, Mahiru, so rest assured."

"Th-there you go again, saying things like that…"

"You seemed like you wanted an explanation. If I didn't say it, you'd probably start getting jealous again."

This time Amane had been whispering quietly enough that other people couldn't hear him. Mahiru pressed her lips tightly closed in frustration, then cast her eyes downward again in embarrassment.

"…I feel stupid for getting anxious about it."

"I don't mind you checking in with me every time until you're satisfied."

"If I actually do that, I'll just get embarrassed."

"Will you be satisfied if I tell you that I love it when you look embarrassed?"

"Are you trying to kill me?"

"That's a bit of an exaggeration."

"No, it's not. My heart is always agonizing over you, Amane, or maybe I should say…it's really hard on me."

"If you don't like it—"

"I don't dislike it, but…I guess I'd like it if you'd, um, go easy on me."

Mahiru squirmed and drew herself inward. Hearing her say such things just made Amane want to tease her more, but if he did it too much she would pout, so he also reasoned that he had better use moderation.

For the time being he answered, "I can do that."

But he could feel dissatisfied eyes glaring at him. He got the sense that he hadn't entirely gained her trust.

"…Next time someone does any tormenting, it's going to be me, okay?"

"I'd be interested to see that."

"…If you're going to do that on purpose, I'm not talking to you."

Mahiru was extremely adorable when she turned away in a huff, and when it made him smile in spite of himself, she snatched away his cookie, looking displeased, before turning her face away again.

Naturally, in such a crowded place, they couldn't linger for a long conversation, so after a reasonable amount of time, they finished up their chat and left the café. Amane let out a sigh, and wondered where they should head next.

The culture festival ran until four o'clock. After about another hour and a half, they would close things down.

Then things would get busy again as the students totaled up their sales, listened to the day's reports, and prepared for the following day. Amane wanted to enjoy himself until then, but they had already visited all of the notable rooms.

"Mahiru, are there any other places you want to go?"

"Let me see…we've already checked out a good amount. What if we go check out the stage in the gym for a little while?"

"The stage, huh? What was it they're doing right now?"

At their culture festival, there was a stage set up in the afternoon, where interested students could put on various performances. Amane remembered that there was a list of live acts and shows written in the schedule.

When he checked the pamphlet, it said that there was currently a live performance by the popular music club going on.

"It says there's a live band right now. You interested?"

"I don't listen to much music, so if they're putting on a whole show—"

"You don't usually turn on any background music, Mahiru, and even if you do, it's always classical music, huh?"

Mahiru was generally sensitive to trends, but she didn't know much about music, or rather, her preferences lay with the classical Western music she liked and listened to, rather than popular Japanese music.

When it came to the famous male pop idols that often appeared on television, Mahiru only seemed to know enough to match up their names and faces.

"Well, if you're interested, Mahiru, let's go. I'd like to see it."

"Sure, okay."

There were no other stands they particularly wanted to visit, so to satisfy their curiosity and kill some time, Amane took Mahiru by the hand and headed for the gymnasium.

It already had most of the lights turned out, and the lights that were on were focused on illuminating the stage.

They'd been able to hear the music from outside the gym, but it was much louder once they were inside. Feeling a tickle from the music that seemed to resonate in their guts, they softly closed the door so as not to bother the other spectators and slipped into an open spot.

When Amane lifted his head, the group that was volunteering at the moment was standing on a platform where they were going to perform their song.

Among them was a face that he recognized. Amane narrowed his eyes and took a closer look.

Standing there in front of the mic stand was a familiar face that Amane had seen many times since that morning.

"…Whoa, that's Kadowaki! He never told me he was performing!"

They had been to karaoke together countless times, so Amane knew what a good singer his friend was, but he had never expected to see him standing on stage like that. Even more so, because he hadn't heard any gossip about it.

Amane was surprised by Yuuta's vitality. In addition to his club activities and preparing for this culture festival, there he was, standing on stage.

However, this was unexpected because Yuuta himself didn't seem to like to attract too much attention.

"Mister Kadowaki really can do anything, can't he?

"You're one to talk, Mahiru."

Mahiru seemed impressed, but she was the same way. She was also basically capable of anything. She could do schoolwork and sports and housework, and all of it at a high level. People as accomplished as Mahiru were quite rare.

"There are things that even I can't do," Mahiru confessed.

"Like?"

"…Swimming."

"I guess that counts. Ultimately, you never did learn to swim, did you?"

"If you think someone can learn to swim in just one day, you're dreaming. No matter how much I practiced, I just never made any progress, but…"

"Sorry."

Mahiru gently pummeled his upper arm with her fists, registering her objection to the way he said she "never learned to swim." Smiling wryly at her reaction, Amane turned his gaze back toward the stage.

Yuuta didn't seem to like to stand out, but he had mentioned before that he was used to getting attention. Even in front of lots of spectators, he didn't look concerned. Confidence oozed from every pore.

He had no problem standing up there wearing a mellow smile, gently waving his hand back and forth at the audience.

And then, the area in front of Yuuta just happened to open up and make it easy for him to see to the back of the crowd. When he met Amane's eye, his cheek twitched faintly.

Apparently he hadn't been expecting them to come.

Swearing he would ask Yuuta about it later, Amane casually waved back, and after blinking a few times, Yuuta put on a completely different smile than before.

When they saw the way his face changed, the girls all shrieked, so both Amane and Mahiru couldn't help but grin.

Same as it ever was, huh?

"Why didn't you tell us you were performing?"

Amane tried to grill Yuuta about it when he came to see them after his number was over, where they were standing by the wall. But Yuuta frowned and laughed awkwardly as he fastened his necktie, which had been open to allow him to sing.

"I wasn't planning to at first, but our vocalist hurt his leg at practice a week ago… As you might expect, the doctor told him not to perform while he had an injury, and I guess you could say I was the pinch hitter."

It was the kind of performance that required moving around a lot, so it certainly would have been impossible with an injury.

"Gotcha. Is the guy who hurt his leg okay?" Amane asked.

"Yeah, he's all right. Of course, he seemed disappointed that he couldn't perform, so that was too bad. But it sounds like he still enjoyed watching it."

"Well, there was no helping it… But, wow, you sang amazing for a pinch hitter! It was perfect."

"Did I? That's good."

Yuuta had always been an outstanding singer, something Amane had experienced personally at their karaoke sessions, but he'd never expected Yuuta to stay so cool standing up on stage in front of an audience. More than that, he captivated the spectators.

Amane had been impressed by his friend's skill as he listened to the cheers from the girls. Yuuta could see that, and scratched his cheek bashfully.

"…Still, this is kind of embarrassing. I guess I feel self-conscious knowing that my friends were watching."

"Would it have been better if we didn't watch?"

"No, that's not what I mean. I see both of you all the time, so it was a little reassuring to have you here. That relief when you see some familiar people in the crowd, you know?"

Yuuta smiled bashfully and said that it had actually been helpful to have them there, and the girls around them, who had been stealthily watching their interaction, burst into a commotion.

Amane silently chuckled at the way his friend always attracted attention wherever he went. He smiled at Yuuta, who was wearing a smile that was equally bashful and proud. "Glad to be of service," he said.

Mahiru simply acknowledged his effort with a gentle smile of her own. "Well done up there," she said, stubbornly maintaining her stance as Amane's companion.

She was probably doing so to prevent unnecessary jealousy from coming her way. It was well-known that Mahiru was dating Amane, but even so, if she acted too friendly with Yuuta in public, it might cause trouble or give the wrong impression.

"But it's too bad," Amane said. "I wish I'd known so I could've brought Itsuki and the others."

"Ah, I'd rather you didn't tell Itsuki. He'll complain that I didn't tell him, and probably make fun of me, too."

"Well, you're just going to have to grin and bear it. It's your fault for keeping it a secret."

"What could I do? It got decided so suddenly. Call it an act of god."

Yuuta was laughing and telling him to drop it, so Amane swore he would say something later when the whole class was assembled. He punched Yuuta lightly on the shoulder with a smile. "Not a chance," he said.

"Great job on day one, everyone! Boy, we really worked hard!"

The stage performances went on until the end of the day, and after watching the rest of the show with Mahiru and Yuuta, Amane returned to their classroom.

The program for day one of the culture festival was over, and his classmates, who had all completed their own shifts, were gathered in the classroom. Amane could tell they'd enjoyed themselves, because it showed on their faces.

When Itsuki expressed his appreciation for their efforts as their festival committee member, Amane's classmates all raised a shout.

After the commotion had settled down somewhat, Itsuki cleared his throat and got their attention again.

"Okay, so now we've gotta get through prep for tomorrow and a little bit of cleanup. Accounting, tally up our sales and the number of orders and check that it matches the cash we have on hand, then report to me. Put the money into the bag they gave us and hand that over to me, too. I'll go turn it in to management. You guys in back of house, get ready for tomorrow, and the hospitality team can clean the classroom. Once you're done with that, go organize equipment in the back."

"Okay!"

Each group had their marching orders and obediently started on their given tasks.

Amane was on cleaning duty, so in order to get it done quickly, he rolled up his sleeves and went to fill up some buckets with water.

A year earlier, he had been the worst of the worst when it came to cleaning, but thanks to Mahiru's guidance and daily practice, he had gotten to the point where it might not be his specialty, but he could get it done with average skill. It was probably more accurate to say that he had gotten to the point where he could maintain a state of cleanliness.

"...You're making quick work of that."

Ayaka spoke up, sounding impressed, when she saw Amane cleaning in sync with Mahiru.

"Oh, no, Mahiru's much better at this than I am. She's basically like my teacher. At first, I really couldn't even pick up after myself."

"I'm surprised to hear that. I always imagined you as a methodical person, Fujimiya."

"You have always acted very mature outside the house, Amane," Mahiru added in a teasing tone of voice. She had apparently been listening to their conversation as she folded and put away the dirty tablecloths.

The only thing Amane could do after she implied that he was slovenly at home was to keep quiet. She was right enough that he couldn't complain, but he didn't like getting made fun of too much.

"It's unavoidable, right? That's just what guys who live alone are like."

"Even so, it was really bad. When I walked into your apartment, there was nowhere to step."

"...That's just how it is."

"Is that so?" Ayaka remarked. "Well, he doesn't live alone, but my sweet Sou keeps a clean room, you know? Since I go in there, he always keeps it perfectly tidy. There's not even anything under the bed!"

"Even so, you should stop poking around."

Most guys would balk at the thought of their girlfriend brazenly looking for things under their bed.

Amane wished that every girl in every couple in the whole country would stop digging up things that were supposed to be hidden.

In Amane's case, there wasn't anything for Mahiru to find, so he wasn't overly concerned. But he figured that most guys *would* mind, and he could only assume it would be problematic if certain things were found.

"Ah, no, I wasn't trying to poke around," Ayaka insisted, "but I was just curious if he had the usual stuff or not. You know, like how it always is in manga?"

"Clearly you've been reading too many."

"Fair, fair. Besides, Sou is way too easy to read... By the way, what about you, Fujimiya?"

"I don't appreciate your groundless suspicions."

"Ah-ha-ha!"

Ayaka cackled with laughter, and Amane was suddenly filled with sympathy for her boyfriend.

Mahiru tilted her head slightly. "What are you two talking about?" she asked.

Mahiru had apparently been busy with her work, and was not following their conversation. She looked at them questioningly, and Amane acted as natural as possible, but averted his eyes.

"Nothing important."

"Hmm, I guess we're talking about something that Fujimiya doesn't need since he has you, Miss Shiina."

"Kido!"

He glared at Ayaka, and yelled at her not to say weird things. Ayaka was smiling impishly, as he held back the shame that came slowly oozing up from the depths.

His glaring only made her smile more. At the same time, Mahiru was standing there blinking, looking even more confused. Amane couldn't stand it any longer, and he took Mahiru by the hand and dragged her away from Ayaka.

Chapter 11

Culture Festival, Day Two

It was the second day of the culture festival.

Amane was on shift in the afternoon, so he was free all morning, but…

"I haven't been to my alma mater in a long time, but it's just like it always was. They've done some reorganizing, but the atmosphere is just the same."

Amane's father, Shuuto, who they hadn't seen since summer, mumbled to himself as he stood in front of the doors looking up at the school building with a smile.

Standing there next to him, or more accurately, snuggled up right beside him, Amane's mother, Shihoko, was also smiling gently. "I suppose we haven't visited since Amane's entrance ceremony," she remarked.

As always, they were being affectionate. Amane was used to it, but it was attracting some attention from the people around them, and Amane wished just a little that he could put some distance between himself and them and pretend like they were not related.

Of course, Mahiru was hanging on his arm, stopping him from going anywhere. The look in her caramel-colored eyes was warm, and told him to resign himself to it, so there was nothing Amane could do.

"…Um, so, do we also have to walk around with you?"

"Oh, how can you say that when we haven't seen you in months?" his mother exclaimed. "What a terrible son you are."

"I'm too old to hang around with my parents."

"Don't be ridiculous… Ah, could this be the sort of hateful rebellion against doing things with your parents that so frequently occurs in adolescence?"

"I don't hate you…you just stand out."

At the present moment, they were very conspicuous.

It was clear to see that the two of them were a youthful and well-matched couple. One rarely saw middle-aged couples that were as flirty as they were.

Amane knew that if his classmates saw them, he would get teased about it later, so if possible, he didn't want to walk around with them.

Mahiru, on the other hand, had apparently never had her parents participate in a school event, and she must have been happy that Shihoko and Shuuto had come, because she seemed to want to walk around with them.

Amane felt guilty disregarding her meager request, since he knew about her family history, and if it would make his girlfriend happy, he was prepared to put up with it, but still, embarrassing things were embarrassing.

"…Do we really stand out?" his mother grumbled. "I think you two are plenty conspicuous yourselves."

Then she looked at Amane and Mahiru, who were snuggled close together, and smiled in satisfaction.

Somehow or other, Amane knew that her look was one of both amusement and encouragement, and he could feel his cheek threaten to start twitching.

"…Even so, between a couple of students and a pair of parents, the parents stand out more."

"Well, that may be true," his mother admitted, "but it doesn't change the fact that you do stand out. In fact, you're showing off, aren't you?"

"We are not… Anyway, listen, you want to go around to the different snack stands, right? Well, we have our shifts this afternoon, so if we're going, let's hurry up."

"Oh, so you're going to come with us?"

"Yeah, as a chaperone."

"I don't know, I think there's a chance that you two might be more passionately in love. Right, Shuuto?"

"Ah-ha-ha, she's right!"

His father's friendly, gentle smile never faded. Amane held his head in his hand and let out a soft sigh.

Unlike his mother, Amane's father didn't tease them, which made things more difficult because Amane couldn't strongly object or argue with him. It would throw the whole mood off, so he couldn't talk back to sharply, or even at all.

"…Just tell me where you want to go first."

"Let's see. We'll get to see where you and Mahiru are working this afternoon, right? So if we set that room aside for the moment, I think I'd like to see some of the shops that are selling handmade goods, since we're here. The pamphlet said that the handicrafts club and the industrial arts club have booths."

"I guess I can show you where those are."

For now, the best thing to do would be to hurry up and fulfill his father's request.

If they stayed where they were, they were just going to needlessly attract even more attention, so ultimately, Amane compromised. He put his arm around Mahiru's back, who was gazing up at him lovingly, and urged her forward with a little push, and they went into the school building.

✳   ✳   ✳

"Your parents are super close, huh, Fujimiya? Just like you guys," Ayaka chuckled.

She was watching Amane's parents, who were looking at the handicraft club's handmade merchandise as they expressed their harmonious relationship with their whole bodies.

Ayaka was working as a shopkeeper. Amane didn't know much about which clubs his classmates belonged to, but apparently Kido was in the handicrafts club, and it was currently her turn to mind the store.

"I was convinced you were the manager of some sports club or something, Kido..."

Amane, who had been keeping a certain distance from his parents, stared at Ayaka, who was wearing an apron that was apparently handmade.

This was a girl who had publicly declared her attraction to muscular bodies and talked about how much she loved muscles all the time, so Amane had been certain that she must be a manager for one of the sports clubs. He'd imagined her taking every opportunity to be where the boys were and look at their muscles, so it was a surprise to find her in the handicrafts club.

"Well, there's nothing illegal about a healthy appreciation for muscles. But unfortunately, I'm flying solo right now. Besides, Sou would get pouty."

"Kayano would?"

"He doesn't think a thing of me looking at guys who are professional bodybuilders on TV or in photographs, but, well, he told me to quit drooling over other students."

"I feel like that's less jealousy and more concern for your reputation, Kido."

Kayano probably didn't want other people seeing a cute girl

gazing spellbound and almost drooling over somebody's muscles. Especially if that girl was his own girlfriend.

But Ayaka seemed to object and puffed out her cheeks sharply.

"How rude! I'm very choosy about who I ogle, you know."

Ayaka insisted that she didn't ogle just any set of pumped-up muscles, but she didn't deny the ogling itself. Instead she put her hands on her hips and threw out her chest.

"Well, I'm in the handicrafts club because my dad's always begging me to please act more ladylike, but... Actually, I guess the main reason is because I get to make clothes for Sou myself, and even take his measurements in person to do that."

"Whoa, you're hardcore..."

"Th-there's nothing wrong with that, is there? I—I mean, look at Miss Shiina, she seems like someone who would personally make you some clothes if you stripped and let her take your measurements."

"Please don't give Mahiru any indecent ideas."

If anything, Mahiru would get embarrassed and refuse to look at Amane's naked body, so she would never want him to strip in the first place. He wouldn't know what to do if she started acting like Ayaka.

Amane did not bother to hide his exasperation when Ayaka looked disappointed for some reason. Just then, Mahiru, who had been looking at crafts with Amane's parents, came over to them and cocked her head questioningly.

"You were deep in conversation over here. What are you talking about?"

"Oh, about how happy you would be if Fujimiya stripped."

"No way that would make her happy. Right, Mahiru?"

"S-something like that would...not, I don't think."

"Why was that such a weak denial?"

He'd expected her to deny it forcefully, with a bright-red face, but her denial had been a little bit hesitant, and Amane couldn't hide his surprise.

"Oh, have I finally convinced Mahiru of the appeal of big muscles?"

"Don't say weird things like that, please. And it would be great if you wouldn't give Mahiru any weird ideas, either."

"All I ever did was talk about how great they are. I'd like it if you would not call the beauty of the human body a 'weird idea'. I think it's offensive to say that admiring the result of someone's hard work building their body and refining their physique is a 'weird idea'."

"Uh, right, sorry."

Ayaka lectured him with an unexpectedly serious face, so he apologized on instinct.

"...Yeah, but even so, what are you going to do if you awaken something in Mahiru?"

"Couldn't you just get naked?"

"I'm not doing that."

He could see that Mahiru was visibly overheating, so he wasn't going to take anything off. He had no doubt that she wouldn't be able to make eye contact with him for a while.

He glared at Ayaka, telling her that not everyone wanted to see naked bodies, but Ayaka didn't look the least bit ashamed. With a grin, she mumbled, "But I bet Miss Shiina would like to see..."

Mahiru, meanwhile, was shaking her head back and forth, and her face was red, so Ayaka was probably being ridiculous, when she imagined that anyone else was like her.

Mahiru, who seemed like she was about to boil over, mumbled, with trembling lips, "I hardly ever even think about such vulgar things."

"Oh, so you *do* think about them at least a little?" Ayaka prodded, and Mahiru zipped her lips up tight.

Amane, for his part, pretended like he didn't hear anything. In Mahiru's case, it was probably because she was interested in her sweetheart. He had to believe that it didn't come out of some prurient interest, like with Ayaka.

"My, my, it looks like you're having a fun conversation!"

While Amane was thinking about how to soothe the bright-red Mahiru, his parents walked over, wearing relaxed smiles. Apparently they had purchased something they liked, and they were putting their purchase in a bag.

Ayaka seemed surprised by their sudden appearance. After blinking several times, she straightened up in her seat, and put on what was probably her best customer service smile. It was a sophisticated one that didn't reveal the slightest hint of the grin she had been wearing during their earlier discussion. Amane couldn't help but freeze up at how completely she had changed her demeanor.

"Ah, you must be Fujimiya's parents. My name is Ayaka Kido, and I'm a classmate of Fujimiya and Miss Shiina."

"Very pleased to meet you. I'm Shuuto Fujimiya. This is my wife, Shihoko."

Amane's father gave his name and introduced Amane's mother. Ayaka bobbed her head with a smile. It was plain to see that she was feigning friendliness, so Amane cracked a smile.

"What were you kids talking about?"

"...About Kido's interests."

His father asked the question, so Amane gave a basic answer while averting his eyes, and his mother got a curious twinkle in her eye.

"Oh, what kind of interests do you have, dear?"

"Let's see, people watching...I guess you could call it? I like watching people who are working hard and cheering them on."

She was appreciating people's bodies, so she wasn't lying. And cheering people on as they exerted themselves, that was certainly about muscles too, so it didn't feel inconsistent. At the same time, it wasn't entirely accurate either.

"So, how is our Amane doing, from your perspective? Is he trying hard?"

"Let me see...I think he is trying his best. However, I haven't actually known him for that long, so I guess I would say Fujimiya is still sort of an unknown quantity..."

Amane was sure he remembered Ayaka talking about his muscles, but he couldn't make a crack about it in front of his parents. It would be unbearable if he accidentally sparked such an embarrassing conversation.

Mahiru must have understood that too, because she was also staying quiet. But in a moment when his parents' attention was captured by the conversation, she stealthily patted Amane's stomach, making him worry that Ayaka might have poisoned her after all.

As he brushed her hand away, he chided her, "Save that for home, please."

Mahiru, who seemed to have realized just what she was doing in front of other people, quickly flushed red.

"From what I can see," Ayaka continued, "Fujimiya seems happy and motivated when he's with Miss Shiina, so I look forward to observing their relationship from close-up."

"Oh, so the two of them are getting on well together at school too?"

"Yes, very much so. So well, in fact, that it's affecting the rest of us who have to watch."

"C'mon, Kido, cut it out with the weird comments."

"Hey, that wasn't weird, just the truth. I just really think you're a very well-matched couple, you know?"

Perhaps as payback for saying that her praise of muscles was weird, Ayaka raved about Amane and Mahiru while wearing an impish grin that was nothing like the smile she had given his parents a moment earlier.

Amane's parents smiled happily. They must have been imagining Amane and Mahiru flirting in class. It made Amane want to get out of there immediately.

Amane was aware that his own face was just as red as Mahiru's had been a moment earlier, and he glared at Ayaka to warn her against saying unnecessary things, but Ayaka wasn't bothered at all.

"Sounds like you've gained the approval of everyone in your class too," his father remarked. "That's wonderful, son."

"Shut up."

When his father congratulated him with a soft, genuine smile, Amane twisted his mouth in an uncomfortable grimace and turned away sulkily.

"Amane, you look dead inside…"

"Gee, I wonder why…"

Shuuto and Shihoko left the handicrafts club's stall behind and started walking around the school again. Mahiru followed behind the two of them at a relaxed pace, holding tightly onto Amane so that he wouldn't run away.

Amane was staring at his parents' backs as they enjoyed themselves, trying to hide how disgruntled he was, but he was wearing a disinterested face.

The looks are making me uncomfortable.

Since he was walking around with his attention-grabbing parents, the stares were especially piercing.

Recently, Amane had gotten somewhat used to having people's eyes on him, and although he still didn't like it, it was part of moving through the world as Mahiru's boyfriend.

But this time, the looks were different.

They weren't looks of jealousy or spite, but rather, they were full of curiosity. Since Amane and Mahiru's faces were well-known, people were staring at them with even more interest.

Amane was just trailing listlessly behind his parents, who were walking ahead, flirting with each other as they visited the various refreshment booths.

Mahiru saw how he was acting and frowned uncomfortably.

"If you hate it that much, we can split up from them...," she suggested.

"I don't hate it or anything, just, my family...when I see them acting like that, I guess I get embarrassed..."

"...You're really not one to talk, Amane, I think you're just like your father."

"In what way?"

"Recently, you've been, well, how do I put this...? Unconsciously, and I know you're my boyfriend, but you've been, like, giving off a particular vibe..."

Mahiru lowered her pink cheeks and stuck her lip out in a little pout as she pointed out that he had been doing things like casually squeezing her hand and putting his arm around her shoulders. Unable to argue, Amane pressed his lips into a straight line.

In fact, they had been flirting in front of people, not excessively, but with restraint. They had been touching a little bit like sweethearts did, but that was apparently weighing on Mahiru's mind. She didn't seem to hate it, but she did seem embarrassed by it.

"...Honestly, y-you could be bolder about it, but, um...I know it'll make my heart pound. I'm glad that you've found your confidence, but because of that, I get flustered sometimes. And then, I get way too worried about the strangest things, and...s-sometimes feel like a loser."

"I think that last part is taking it too far."

"But—"

"So then what do you think of me?"

He was greatly troubled by the thought that Mahiru might still consider him a loser, but, well, since they had been dating for a whole four months and hadn't done anything more than kissing, if she said he was a loser, then he must be a loser.

But he had thought that they both wanted to wait, and that Mahiru understood it was a choice he was making because he wanted to treasure her.

But Amane was unhappy that she thought moving so slowly was his standard.

"Sorry for being so slow."

"I-I'm not trying to pressure you, and I know that you're taking your time precisely because you want to be careful. But I think you're worrying about me too much, Amane, and putting yourself last, so... I wonder if that isn't difficult for you?"

Although Mahiru was inexperienced, and knew even less than Amane about relations between the sexes, he figured she must be aware of the physiological responses that were typical in men, and that she must have actually noticed those responses in the course of spending time with him.

Amane guessed that she had worded her question so carefully because she knew how he felt, and what's more, because she understood that he hadn't done anything because he respected her and wasn't going to force her into anything.

From Amane's perspective, it was humiliating to have her worry about his feelings like that, plus he was just fully realizing his inexperience, which kept him from exercising enough self-restraint. But he was glad that Mahiru didn't perceive that as a bad thing.

"I'd be lying if I said it wasn't difficult, but listen, I... If you're happy, Mahiru, then I'm happy...I don't think we have to rush ahead or anything."

"...Please realize that I am also happy if you're happy, Amane."

"That's why your happiness is the most important."

"We're just going around in circles, aren't we?"

With a discontented look, she poked her fingertip into his side repeatedly, but it wasn't enough to change his feelings.

He looked down at Mahiru's disapproving face and smiled softly to tell her that he wasn't going to budge, which prompted her to make an even more disapproving expression, so to pacify her, he tickled the hand he was holding with one fingertip.

"You don't need to worry about me, Mahiru."

"...That's one of the irritating things about you, Amane."

"Well, there's nothing I can do about that."

He made this assertion, implying that he wasn't going to budge, and with an expression that was difficult to read—not angry, but containing exasperation and a little bit of irritation—Mahiru head-butted Amane's upper arm.

"So you also understand how cute my darling Mahiru is, right?"

"Oh, of course I do! Sweet Mahiru has plenty of charms...the more I get to know her, the cuter she is."

Although they had just met for the first time that day, Amane's mother Shihoko and his friend Chitose were kindred spirits. They were admiring Mahiru together. Watching them talk just made Amane let out a huge sigh.

"You two are a dangerous mix..."

Itsuki and Chitose were on the same café shift with Amane that day, so they were also free to move about during the morning. Everything had been going well until Amane's group had run into them by chance and, unavoidably, he had introduced his parents.

That was when the problems started. At first, Chitose had quietly behaved herself, but once Amane's mother had started doting on Mahiru, Chitose hadn't been able to hold herself back, and had joined in.

From there, they'd very quickly realized their affinity, and ultimately Mahiru ended up trembling with bright-red cheeks as the two of them praised this and that about her.

Her caramel-colored eyes, welling up with embarrassment, were looking to Amane for help. But there was no way he could triumph against Chitose and his mother working together, so for the time being, he let them do as they pleased, and took refuge with the other males.

"Thank you for looking after our Amane," Amane's father said.

"Nothing to it," Itsuki replied.

"...Geez."

"What's the matter, Amane? You aren't going to deny it, are you?"

"It's a fact that you do try to help me out. Whether your help is needed, and whether it actually improved anything, is a different question."

Occasionally, Itsuki did meddle where it was none of his business, but generally he was helpful and did look after Amane. Amane did feel a debt of gratitude to him, and he rarely said so, but he appreciated Itsuki every day.

If Itsuki hadn't been around, his relationship with Mahiru probably never would have progressed. In a sense, Itsuki came in a set with Chitose, and they could be considered key figures in his courtship with Mahiru.

He was grateful to his friend, so he didn't deny father's words, and for some reason, Itsuki averted his eyes.

"You sure can be honest about things like that, man."

"Are you trying to start a fight about how I'm usually too sulky?"

"Taking it that way is the very definition of sulky, you know. Wait, so you knew that you were acting that way this whole time?"

"Shut up, you jerk," Amane slapped him on the back, but he was just fooling around a little, so Itsuki didn't try to stop him. Instead, he grinned and looked over at Amane's family.

Even Amane's father was giving him an amused smile. Amane couldn't stand it, but when he turned away, he could still hear their smiles in their voices as they spoke.

"Well, Amane can be sulky, and he's not very upfront about his feelings, but I think he's an honest guy."

"Amane's always been like that, you know. He's always had a hard time letting people get close, but I'm glad that he has a friend who understands him."

"No, no, I'm the one who should be glad that I get to be his friend.

"…Do you think you two could maybe talk about this when I'm not around?"

"But—"

"Right, okay then, we'll talk later over text…"

Amane had meant that he didn't want to listen to their conversation, but the way things unfolded, Itsuki and Shuuto somehow started exchanging contact information. Amane felt a headache coming on. It seemed like they were opening a secret back channel through which anything he did would be reported to his father, so he wished they would stop.

However, even if he put a stop to it, Chitose and Shihoko seemed likely to conspire to do something anyway, so he felt a keen hunch that trying to interfere was pointless.

No matter what I do, Mahiru and I are going to get made fun of…

He knew that his parents and friends would probably talk about them with affection, but the thought was still unbearable.

Thinking that he had better warn them all off gossiping later, he looked away—and there, in the corner of his vision, he spotted Itsuki's father, Daiki, who he had also met the day before.

Daiki was a parent, so it wasn't strange that he would come to both days of the festival, but he didn't seem like he was going to come over and speak to them. He was just watching them from afar with a troubled look on his face. Amane was confused.

Daiki's gaze was directed toward Itsuki, so perhaps he was worried about his son.

"Amane, what's...?"

Itsuki noticed Amane looking worried, and when he also turned to look, his handsome face stiffened.

Amane knew that father and son were not on good terms by any means, but as Itsuki's friend, seeing such an obvious response made Amane extremely uncomfortable.

He looked at Itsuki, wondering what to do. Itsuki's lips were trembling like he had something to say, but that never turned into words. Instead he turned away and pretended not to see his father.

Itsuki walked straight over to Chitose, who was still chatting excitedly, and flashed a big grin.

"Chi, let's go buy some food soon, yeah? If we don't get in line soon, we'll be working hungry this afternoon."

"Uh-oh, we don't want that. Not when serving customers takes so much stamina. Ah, sorry, but we'll be going now."

"Oh? Well, we're planning to come to your café this afternoon, so we'll see you then."

"Yes, we're looking forward to it."

Chitose bowed politely, and they left. Itsuki was subtly hurrying her along. Chitose's expression probably would have soured if she had noticed Daiki, but still, Amane couldn't help but feel like Itsuki was being too blatant about his feelings toward his father.

...How did they get to this point, I wonder?

Amane let out a soft sigh at Itsuki, who was ignoring Daiki as if he wasn't there.

"...Sorry for the trouble."

After watching to make sure that Itsuki and Chitose had left, Daiki, who had been watching them from afar, approached Amane, wearing a bitter smile.

Even for Amane, it was a supremely uncomfortable situation, but still, it wasn't like he could poke his nose too deeply into their problems, so he just watched his friends leave.

Amane's mother seemed to notice Daiki approaching, and she walked up to him with Mahiru in tow.

Amane introduced him. "This is Itsuki's father."

"Is he now? Our son owes a lot to your son Itsuki."

"Oh, no, I'm sure it's the other way around..."

Watching his parents and Daiki introduce themselves after their normal parental humility contest, Amane felt incredibly awkward.

"...Ah, but, Daiki, what just happened?"

"I was expecting it. I've always given Itsuki's girlfriend a hard time, so Itsuki keeps his distance. I get it."

Daiki accepted the situation matter-of-factly. He seemed more resigned than sad. Shuuto and Shihoko both seemed to pick up on the fact that Daiki's relationship with Chitose, his son Itsuki's girlfriend, was not good, and they frowned, looking a little concerned.

While chatting with his parents, Amane had previously mentioned that two of his friends were having a hard time because their parents didn't approve of their relationship, so they probably remembered that conversation.

Daiki didn't appear to pay any attention to Amane's parents' reaction, and after looking into the distance as if recalling the scene from a moment earlier, he smiled a little.

"But, wow, you're really on good terms with Fujimiya's parents, Miss Shiina. I'm surprised to see that."

"Thank you for your kind words."

"Of course, she's our future daughter-in-law. Even if she wasn't, she's a good girl, and she's easy to pamper."

That was partially because of Shihoko's and Shuuto's personalities. And also, since Amane's relationship with Mahiru had his parents' official approval, he thought it was only natural that they would try to get along with his partner and their future daughter-in-law. But Amane had been hesitant to say that, since it might sound like a dig at Daiki, but…his mother didn't seem worried when she declared it without reservation.

Amane thought that maybe she had done it on purpose, but there seemed to be more thought behind it than he first assumed. His father also didn't make any attempt to stop her. It was clear that she didn't mean anything bad by it, she was just genuinely smitten with Mahiru.

Listening to her talk, Mahiru looked embarrassed, and Daiki's eyes opened wide like he was taken aback. Then a beat later, he put on a strained smile.

"Well, with her, I suppose the two of you don't have any complaints at all."

"That's certainly true. Because she is the person our son has chosen. His judgment didn't fail him, and when we met our darling Mahiru, we knew that she was someone we could trust with Amane."

Amane felt some objection to the idea that he was being entrusted to anybody, but it was a fact that she did look after him, so he couldn't complain.

"I really envy you," Daiki said. "It didn't work out like that for my foolish son."

"You don't trust your son's judgment?"

"My son isn't the accomplished heir that he needs to become, you see. He's just a kid, with a long, long way to go."

"Oh my, I don't think that's quite right. From what Amane tells us, your son seems like a very considerate and kind young man."

"Well..."

Daiki was hesitant to go on. Shihoko smiled at him calmly.

Maybe she was feeling something as a fellow parent, because normally she wouldn't have pressed the issue so far, but this time, Amane's mother wasn't holding back.

They had just watched Itsuki run away from his father to protect his girlfriend, and that was probably why she was acting like this.

"I understand that as a parent, there are certain qualities you hope for in the partner your child chooses, but...children rebel if you restrain them too much, after all. Considering you worked so hard to raise such a lovely son, I think one of your duties as an adult is to trust his judgment and see what happens."

Shihoko told Daiki that with a smile, and Daiki made a sour face as if he had swallowed something bitter. It wasn't a hateful expression; rather, it looked like she had touched a sore spot.

Amane looked at his mother, who didn't appear to have anything further to say, and put on a faintly bitter smile, like his father, Shuuto.

"Now, we just met you, and we have no right to speak out of turn, but...if you try to keep a child from walking down a path they've chosen for themselves, even if it's clearly an error, they'll never listen to you."

Shuuto stared at Daiki with the same pleasant smile as Shihoko as he brought the argument to a close, and Amane scratched his cheek and sighed softly.

Amane didn't really think that it was the sort of conversation that he ought to butt into. But he understood that, for better or worse, Daiki was stubborn, and he also knew that the situation as seen from a parent's perspective was different from the way it looked to the couple in question.

If Daiki already understood that Chitose was not a bad person, that meant there was a disconnect between perception and expectation.

"Please let me say one thing, too," Amane added. "Um, well...I know that you don't think very highly of Chitose, but...she's not a bad person. Recently, she's been working hard and trying to get your approval. I'm not going to tell you to accept her or anything, but... please, take a closer look at her."

Daiki's standards were very high, but there was nothing about Chitose that made her incapable of meeting them. She wasn't stupid or anything, and she was someone who could read the room when it was important. And she could be kind and considerate.

It was simply that Daiki and Chitose had different values, that was all, and he didn't want Daiki to ignore everything that was good about her.

Daiki gazed for a moment in wonderment after Amane's hesitant statement, then looked away awkwardly.

"...I understand, young Fujimiya, that you hold my son in high regard, and that you have confidence in his girlfriend. I also know about the efforts that they have been making. And I understand that a child is not his parent. And yet—"

"And yet?"

"—I don't think that she has had a good influence on my son. Even accepting that my delinquent son has had a good impact on you, that doesn't change my perception of her. That's what I need you to understand."

Amane's words, if he had to say, came from a place of support for Itsuki. He wanted to support his friend, no matter what. He hadn't really considered Daiki's feelings.

Amane knew that the man's feelings weren't going to change just because an outsider like Amane said one thing or another, but…to have his input rejected, however gently, to his face, made his chest hurt just a little.

…I knew that this was an issue that was beyond me, but…

Ultimately, this was an issue between Daiki, Itsuki, and Chitose, and Amane could never truly know what Daiki thought of them.

Without peeking into the man's heart, there was no way to know exactly why he wasn't able to accept Chitose.

"You don't need to worry, young Fujimiya, I'm not scheming to get rid of her. I just have my own way of thinking, and I simply cannot approve of her. You can understand that, surely?"

"…I'm sorry, that was too forward of me, it wasn't my place."

"No, I'm glad that my son has made a friend like you. Because you seem to genuinely care about him."

Daiki didn't seem upset. He just put on a faint smile with a little bitterness mixed in, and passed his gaze over each member of Amane's party with calm eyes.

"Never mind about me, I want you to continue being good friends with my son, if you would."

Daiki told him this in a firm, heartfelt voice, and lowered his head a little, then left quietly, leaving Amane and his family bewildered.

Even though he understood that Daiki had his own way of thinking about things, Amane let out a heavy sigh that carried inexpressible feelings of disappointment, exasperation, and sadness at things not going the way he had hoped.

"…Amane, usually you're rather short with Mister Akazawa and Chitose, but at times like that, you really stand up for them, don't you?"

After they had lunch, Amane and Mahiru split off from his parents for a while. They had finished changing clothes in preparation for their afternoon shift, and were waiting in the break room for their work to start in about twenty minutes' time.

"…I mean, yeah, they're my friends."

"You're not very up-front about your feelings, you know?"

"Oh, hush. I'm up-front with you, aren't I?"

"I don't know if I'd call it up-front, maybe blunt…sometimes, you astound me so much it's shocking, and it sends my heart racing."

"I'm glad to hear I can get your heart racing."

"Oh, you!"

Mahiru started slapping him. It was more like she was fed up with him than actually unhappy, and Amane shrugged.

"Well, as you saw, I don't push it too far when I stand up for Itsuki and Chitose. They would both hate that. Besides, I know what Daiki wasn't saying."

"What he wasn't saying?"

"Mm…so, their family is pretty wealthy. I don't think you've ever been there, Mahiru, but their house is kind of a mansion."

"A mansion…really?"

"Right, a mansion. Like a real classic Japanese manor house."

Amane had been surprised the first time he had gone over to hang out at Itsuki's invitation. Amane had thought that his own house was large, but still it was no match for a luxurious Japanese mansion with its own detached outbuildings, a pond with a bridge, and well-kept gardens.

Itsuki himself had sounded a little embarrassed about his "musty old house," as he'd put it, but to Amane, it seemed less old-fashioned and more historical. He thought it was a handsome place, undamaged and well cared for over the years.

"Anyway, he comes from that kind of family. Apparently he's got a brother who's pretty much an adult already, and his brother will be inheriting the house, but that doesn't change the fact that Itsuki is the second son of a prestigious family."

"…I see."

"Well, Itsuki claims that since he's the second son and not the heir, he can do whatever he wants. He says he doesn't want his parents putting limits on who he can date."

Amane could understand Itsuki's insistence, and also how he wouldn't want his parents deciding something like that for him despite being at an age where he could think for himself.

However, he hadn't gotten the sense from seeing Daiki earlier that his rejection of Chitose was entirely because of her influence over Itsuki. Amane had a feeling that there was some other main reason why he would not accept Chitose.

He would probably never know unless he asked Daiki directly, but it was also obviously not the sort of thing that he thought the man was likely to talk about.

Even so, it wasn't great that he wouldn't listen to the two people at the center of the issue. Amane wasn't inclined to take Daiki's side.

"I know that Itsuki's dad probably has his own way of thinking about things, but, you know, from where I stand, considering that forcing them apart will make them rebel and give rise to more friction, I think things would be easier going forward, both practically and emotionally, if he would compromise with them a little."

Amane concluded with a shrug, conceding that it wasn't his place to talk, since he wasn't one of the people involved. Mahiru stared fixedly at Amane, then her face softened into a loving smile.

"…I'm feeling a little jealous of Mister Akazawa."

"Jealous?"

When he heard that completely unexpected word, his eyes widened automatically.

As for Mahiru, she prefaced what she was about to say with an awkward smile. "This might be inappropriate, but…," she began. Then she sighed softly as she expressed her thoughts on the matter.

"I don't think it's an unbearable situation from their perspective, Amane. Even though they don't agree, Itsuki's father is still thinking about what's best for him and trying to protect him, right? There's no denying that he's prioritizing his own values, but…even so, that's still a form of parental love."

When she said the words *parental love*, it made him stiffen, slightly enough that he hoped she didn't notice.

"Ah, you don't have to worry about me."

Mahiru smiled faintly. Apparently she had noticed Amane's concern. She played with a bit of her hair, winding it around her fingers, and gently cast her eyes downward.

"At this point, I'm not expecting anything from my parents. But you know, seeing them and thinking about the tenuous relationship that I have with my family, I do feel jealous. Well, even if my family reached out to me, I don't think I would accept their offer at this point."

She added quietly that she already considered that link severed, and twirled her hair into a tight spiral.

In response to this gesture, which seemed to be occupying her attention somewhat, Amane carefully reached out and unwound the lock of silky hair from her fingers. Then he went straight on to gently stroke her cheek.

Mahiru gazed up into his eyes.

Amane could see that her eyes were wavering slightly, but decided not to point that out, and smiled calmly back at her.

"Well, you've got my parents, Mahiru, so you kind of get to experience it, in a way. My parents always say that all their affection is wasted on me anyway."

Mahiru was already like a daughter to the Fujimiya family.

What's more, Amane's parents fawned over her even more than their biological son. His parents were aware that Mahiru was starved for love, which only made them dote on her more.

Mahiru blinked dramatically several times at Amane's words, then as his meaning sunk in, she slowly broke into a broad smile.

"...Heh-heh, that's not true. You're wonderful, Amane."

"Thank you very much... You are loved, so you don't need to be so anxious about it."

"Okay."

Looking a little bashful, Mahiru leaned in close to Amane, who was by her side. Amane also smiled a little, and accepted her into his arms, and they quietly cuddled close together for a little while.

Chapter 12

A Blessed Relationship with the Angel

"Oh my, Mahiru honey, that's a very cute costume!"

When it was time for their shift, Amane's parents showed up right away, and Amane went out to greet them with Mahiru, forcing his twitching cheeks into a smile along the way.

His mother's eyes visibly lit up when she saw Mahiru in her maid outfit, and she started enthusiastically looking the outfit over, and actually touching it to see what it was like.

Mahiru must have already been used to the attention, because all she did was put on a strained smile, but as a rule, she was supposed to turn his mother down. No matter how well they were acquainted, once Amane's mother set that precedent in a public space, people would misunderstand and keep doing the same thing. They didn't want that.

Mahiru had given in to his mother's boldness, and was letting her do as she pleased, so Amane sighed and reached out to hold his mother back.

"Ma'am, please refrain from touching our maids."

"Well, I suppose this is your personal maid."

"Any normal person would know that I meant the café's maids!"

©Hanekoto

His mother tried to take his words to mean that Mahiru was his own maid, which set Amane's cheek twitching again. But his mother didn't seem to care, and Amane sensed that there would be no point in trying to put on a good front. Instead, he decided to be direct with her.

"My, my, what a sharp tongue this employee has… By the way, am I not allowed to touch her because you're too possessive?"

"No, it's because those are the rules! Touching is strictly prohibited. We do not offer that type of service here. Please stop, so that you don't set a bad example for the other customers."

"That even applies to her mother?"

"Stop it. And you aren't her mother yet."

Shihoko probably already thought of herself as Mahiru's mother figure. Actually, she was more like a mother to her than Mahiru's real mother was, and what's more, Mahiru had received a lot more affection from Shihoko than her actual son, Amane, did. But even so, Mahiru was still only her son's girlfriend.

Amane was less interested in shoving that fact in her face than he was in showing his parents to their table. Several other groups of customers had been glancing over at them during their conversation. Even their classmates were looking at them, so they were clearly making fools of themselves.

"Oh, that's fine, it doesn't change anything either way."

"Listen…that's enough. Whatever you say, just let me take you to your seats."

"Of course, there are still other customers, after all. I suppose we can have you take us in. Lead the way, sir."

Amane's lips were trembling with irritation at his mother, who was grinning broadly at him. But his father, who had been silent through the whole thing, was apologizing with his eyes. Amane secretly let a sigh slip out as he suppressed his feelings and put on his customer service persona.

"Pardon me, ma'am. I will now show you to your table."

Attempting to smooth things over, Amane ignored his mother's grin and led the two of them to an open table. Mahiru had gone back to serving other customers, and was taking orders at another table.

Amane wondered why he had to face his parents in this getup, and nearly sighed from the shame. But he held it in, and showed them the menu.

"Here is our menu. Please note that everything is sold in sets."

"Oh, is that so? Shuuto, what will you have?"

"Let me see, what's the staff recommendation?"

"If the customer prefers coffee, I recommend the A set. If tea is better, I would suggest the C set instead."

His father wasn't teasing him like his mother, but it was still tough to have him looking at him with amusement in his eyes. Amane had been fine serving his other classmates, but he felt embarrassed now that he was serving a family member.

His mother was grinning foolishly, so he was already plenty irritated, though.

"Oh, and I'd like a maid to take home."

"That service is not offered at our café."

"But you get to take one home, Amane."

"I do not understand what you are talking about, ma'am. Now, what would you like to order?"

With a cheerful smile, Amane ignored her comment and firmly implied that he had no intention of continuing that conversation. His mother stuck her lip out in a disappointed pout.

Given her age, she had no business making such an immature gesture, but even though she was his mother, it didn't make him feel awkward or uncomfortable, and it ultimately just came off as playful, which was impressive in its own way.

"Right, okay then, I think we'll get one each of sets A and C. That should be good, don't you think, Shihoko?"

"Yes. That way we can enjoy them both. That's so like you, Shuuto."

"Your tastes haven't changed one bit from back then, Shihoko."

"Certainly, please wait a moment."

After taking their order, Amane immediately left them. He was fully aware that no matter what, they were about to start flirting.

Sure enough, he could hear them talking like sweethearts behind him, so he let out a soft sigh as he went to relay their orders to the back, only to find one of his classmates staring at him intently.

"One A set and one C set... What?"

"Are those your parents, Fujimiya?"

"...Unfortunately."

"What do you mean, unfortunately? ...Man, you and your mom have totally different personalities."

His classmate must have noticed his mother's cheerfulness. In comparison, Amane must have seemed nothing like her at all.

His classmate glanced out at the front, at his parents smiling as they conversed at their table, then looked back at Amane.

"...Ah—"

"What? What's that 'ah' for?"

"Well, I guess you do take after them. Your dad anyway."

"Oh yeah? Well, I do think I look more like my dad than my mom, but..."

"Uh-huh, yeah, you do."

That response made it seem like his classmate had more to say. Amane narrowed his eyes, but before he could press them about it, his classmate said, "Gotta go!" and hurried away. Amane went back to his post, wondering what that was all about.

*　　*　　*

Thanks to the strange attention they were getting from his classmates, Amane ended up carrying his parents' orders to their table himself. But for some reason, his parents had gotten ahold of Yuuta.

Judging by Yuuta's expression, they seemed to be chatting amiably, but Amane couldn't help but worry that they might put some weird ideas in his head.

His father was there to keep things in check, so Amane didn't think that his parents were likely to disclose anything that would have a bad impact later. But even his father could be careless sometimes, so it wasn't a guarantee that they wouldn't say anything uncalled-for.

Amane moved as quickly as he was able while making sure not to shake the things that were on his tray. "Here is your order," he said in a monotone voice after he set their food down on the table.

He glared at his parents, not bothering to hide the look in his eyes that asked what they were up to, and only got smiles in return. His glaring didn't seem to have any effect.

Yuuta blinked a few times at Amane's demeanor, then put on a gentle smile.

"Kadowaki, what are you doing...?" Amane asked.

"I thought I'd bring them their water and say hello while I was here."

He was holding a carafe of ice water in his hands, so he probably wasn't lying.

"And let me just say, your mother is certainly a beauty, Fujimiya."

"Goodness, what flattery! Yuuta, you're quite the charmer, though you're no match for my Shuuto."

"Ah-ha-ha, I'm honored."

She had called Yuuta casually by his first name, and Amane broke into a cold sweat wondering when they had become such good friends. But all three of them were in a genial mood and didn't seem to notice Amane's panic.

"Thank you for getting along so well with our son. That boy can be blunt, and he has a bit of a sharp tongue, doesn't he?"

"No, not at all. Sure, he never smiles much, but he expresses his emotions in his own way, and although his words can be a little harsh at times, he absolutely never has anything bad to say about anyone. I think he's kind, and a good guy. Besides, recently, he's stopped making sour faces all the time. I think that's thanks to Miss Shiina."

"Well..."

"H-hey, I'm begging you, stop it. This is humiliating."

"Huh, but it's the truth..."

"Whether or not it's true, you don't say those things in front of the person you're talking about."

Yuuta didn't usually poke fun at him, so Amane thought that he was probably being earnest and telling the truth, but hearing it directly from him, and what's more, having his parents hear it, was unavoidably embarrassing.

Amane's father had also had a similar exchange with Itsuki, so it seemed like this day was the day Amane would taste complete humiliation in front of all his friends.

"But you don't accept compliments unless I make it a point to look directly at you and praise you. It's nice to hear sometimes, right?"

"It is not. If you're going to do that, it would be better to tell me directly, and not say anything to my parents."

"Would it? Well then, thanks for everything. I'm glad that I'm your friend."

"...Thanks."

He couldn't reject Yuuta's words, especially when he said them with such a friendly smile. Amane responded with a groan, and when his parents saw how he was acting, his mother spoke up cheerfully.

"The important thing is that you're getting along."

"Quiet, you. And Kadowaki, go back to work, please."

"I guess I'd better. Sorry for taking up your time, see you again later."

The words *see you again* scared him a little, but Yuuta left with the carafe in one hand, still grinning.

Amane was exhausted, weighed down by the heaviest burden of fatigue he had felt that day.

"You seem to have plenty of friends, Amane."

"Yeah, I guess I do..."

He was already worn out and didn't even have the willpower to resist, so he just answered his mother's delighted observation without giving it much thought.

It was the truth that he was blessed with good friends, but that was one thing, and this was another. He wasn't feeling particularly blessed when he was this embarrassed.

Amane made a sulky face, and his father smiled wryly as he picked up his coffee that was on the table.

"Well, you may consider this to be needless meddling, but we were worried about you. You've been living away from home for a year and a half now, and it's good to see things are going well."

It seemed like Amane's father was, in his own way, checking out the people in Amane's life out of concern for him. But even so, Amane would have liked him to stop meddling with his friends so much. Although, those friends had approached his parents themselves, so there was nothing to be done about that.

"It seems like you're opening yourself up to your classmates, and actually, they've all had high opinions of you, along with Miss Shiina."

"They definitely said that stuff today because you two are here, though."

"Well, sorry about that. Though it's probably too late to apologize."

"Just stop talking."

Recently, just being with Mahiru, he had gotten a lot of attention, so in a certain sense, it was probably too late to change anything. But even so, that didn't mean that he wanted to be on the receiving end of those looks.

He shot his father a sharp look, but he got a friendly, tender grin back in return, and Amane turned away; he just couldn't deal with it.

Chapter 13

The End of the Culture Festival and the After-Party

"I'm so tired..."

Amane let out a big sigh as he listened to the announcement of the end of the culture festival that was being broadcast throughout the school.

After his parents had left the café, Amane had been teased by his classmates. He'd had a terrible time. His nerves had already been on edge performing the unfamiliar customer service role, and as his classmates had their fill of teasing him, he had built up a lot of exhaustion, more mental than physical.

However, that seemed to be over now, and as the announcement played again, Amane could feel his shoulders relax.

"All right. Great work, everybody! We were so busy. What a crazy event."

Itsuki checked that there were no more customers and listened to the announcement again, then with a big grin, gathered up his classmates.

Welcoming the end of the culture festival, which had felt both short and long, all of the students were wearing expressions full of accomplishment. However, their exhaustion was also visible, probably because their class had been slammed from beginning to end.

"First of all, before we start thanking everyone, let's clean up.

Honestly, cleanup is the hardest part, it takes even more work than getting ready. It sounds like the school is going to pick up the garbage and dispose of it all at once, so I've been notified that we need to hurry up and collect our trash."

"Ugh."

"Man, what a pain."

The moment the subject of cleanup was raised, it produced a disheartened and listless mood in his classmates. Smiling wryly at how transparent they were, Amane switched into cleanup mode, and listened to them talk as he shoved the trash that had piled up while the café was open into a bag.

"Now, now, if we can just get through this, we can party as much as we want. And we get the day off tomorrow to make up for it. So hurry up and get to work."

"You help, too."

"I am working! I'm...directing. Ow, okay fine, don't hit me!"

Itsuki was standing in front of the blackboard with his chest puffed out self-importantly. Their classmates began to prod him. Itsuki must have been used to having people poke at him. He cracked a smile and joined in the cleanup effort.

"I'll collect the fees for the party after it's over, okay? Nobody tell me that you used all your money at the culture festival yesterday and today!"

"Crap, I wonder if I have enough money left."

"You're the one who put your name on the list to participate, didn't you? Anyone who doesn't have enough cash can borrow from someone else, or get a loan from me, your choice, but you're not gonna believe the interest, it's a hundred percent a day!"

"What kind of rip-off is that?!"

"If you don't like it, then hurry up with the cleaning, and I'll cut you a deal on the interest."

"You better clean, too, Itsuki."

As another classmate smacked him on the shoulder, Itsuki pumped his fist in the air and encouraged everyone to finish up quickly so they could get to the party.

Smirking at his friend, Amane tossed lots of used disposable cutlery into his trash bag. Mahiru was also watching Itsuki as she cleaned alongside him.

"Itsuki's really got a lot of energy, huh?"

"That's just how he is."

"Where's the after-party again?"

"He said he reserved several karaoke rooms. And there's an optional after-party afterward, too."

The after-party was for the people who had expressed interest in attending in advance. The year before, Amane had simply not attended, but this year it wasn't just Itsuki—Mahiru and Chitose would be there too, and he wanted to deepen his friendship with his other classmates as well. So although he felt a little shy about it, he had decided to participate.

Honestly, he wasn't good at singing in front of other people, and if possible he would have preferred to just listen. But Amane knew that Itsuki was likely to force a microphone into his hand, so he was worried about what was going to happen.

"I don't really mind staying out a little late," Amane said, "but you know, I don't handle crowds all that well. I might just go to karaoke and then go home for the day."

Amane's parents were planning to stay in a hotel for several days, so there was no need for him to hurry home. He really wouldn't have minded them staying at his place for just a few nights, but his mother had said, "We would feel bad getting in the way of your canoodling with sweet Mahiru. Besides, you wouldn't like it if I snuggled up to Shuuto in your house, now would you?"

So he had taken her at her word, accepting that—although half if it was none of her business, the other half was welcome consideration—and gladly agreed with her suggestion.

Also, as far as Amane was concerned, getting teased for the way he normally spent time with Mahiru was something he'd gotten quite enough of when they had visited his home over summer break. He had already suffered through it over and over. If he could avoid going through that again, he wanted to.

"That's my plan, too," Mahiru said. "I've already prepared stuff for dinner anyway."

"You're so efficient."

"If you want to reduce the amount of work when you get home, that's what you have to do."

Amane was impressed as Mahiru told him this with a smile, as if it was the most natural thing in the world. He swore in his heart that he would reach that level of forethought himself, but first he steeled his resolve to finish the cleaning that was right there in front of him.

After they finished picking up, Amane and the others were understandably tired, but they still made it to the party.

Itsuki had reserved three karaoke rooms, so the participants broke into groups, and each took one room. This was considerate of Itsuki, so that the people who knew each other well could stick together.

Amane's group obviously included the people he talked to all the time. Starting with Mahiru, it also included Itsuki and Chitose, Yuuta, Kazuya, and Makoto, and Ayaka, who he had just recently started talking with.

All the girls seemed somewhat disappointed that Yuuta was in Amane's group, but they also seemed reassured by the fact that he was in the same room with girls that already had boyfriends and didn't have their eye on him. The girls who ended up in the other rooms grinned as they told Amane, "Make out with Miss Shiina as much as you want, okay?" and Amane answered them with a scowl.

"All right then, good work everyone!"

Following Itsuki's lead as he raised the cup that he had filled with cider at the drink bar in a toast, everyone else in the room raised their own cups.

They were far enough apart that it was hard to bump the cups together, so they ended up just holding that pose for a moment.

After everyone had toasted, Amane took a sip of his melon soda. The unique flavor and aroma was typical of junk food, something that Amane quite enjoyed. But when he let Mahiru have a sip of it like she wanted, wrinkles formed on her brow; it didn't seem to suit her tastes. A big part of that was probably that she didn't love carbonated drinks.

With tears in her eyes, Mahiru sipped her own oolong tea, and snuggled up right next to Amane. She probably did that because she was tired, but also, she must have been anxious about singing karaoke in front of so many people.

"No, but seriously, thanks for all your hard work. This year's VIP is Kido, for real."

After downing a sip of his cider, Itsuki plunked down into his seat, and nodded cheerily.

When she heard her name come up, Ayaka flashed an awkward smile as she took little sips of her water.

"More like the owner of my café. He was so generous to loan us the costumes…though I was surprised that he had so many to spare."

"I'll have to bring him some treats some time to say thank you."

"It's rare to see you taking something so seriously, Itsuki."

"Chi, how can you be so rude to me? I can be serious sometimes."

"How often?"

"…Like once or twice a year maybe?"

"Wow!"

Watching the people around him break into excited laughter, Amane exhaled calmly.

Even if these were all people he knew, he somehow didn't feel like saying anything when there were this many of them. Since he wasn't naturally cheerful like Itsuki, he didn't have great communication abilities, and unless the conversation came around to him, he wasn't particularly inclined to join in.

Mahiru was being herself, watching the excitement with a peaceful look on her face. Lively crowds weren't her cup of tea either, but she also didn't seem to dislike this situation, and was probably having the most fun watching them just like this.

"...Why are you sitting back like this has got nothing to do with you, Amane? Quit making out back there, and you get up here, too."

"I know, I know, I'm coming to you, don't stand up. It's a tight fit in here."

He had gotten them to go ahead and make a little bit of room, but there were eight people in there, so it was hard to move, and the space felt cramped. If they wandered around too much, they would be in each other's way, so really he wished everyone would settle down.

"Mahiruuu, c'mere! Come tease Itsuki."

"No teasing, thank you very much... Miss Shiina, don't tell me you don't like karaoke?"

"N-no, I wouldn't say I dislike it..."

Mahiru squirmed and made herself smaller, and Chitose gave a knowing, "Ah," and directed her gaze upward as she continued.

"...Mmm. I bet Mahiru simply doesn't have much of a song repertoire, so she doesn't want to sing much, that's all. She told me once that the only songs she listened to were either piano songs, or Western songs with lyrics that would help with her English language studies."

"Shows how she was raised… That's exactly what I would expect from Miss Shiina."

"You don't listen to anything with Amane?"

"I'm not really the type to have music playing."

For what it was worth, he did have a sound system sitting in his living room, but it was basically decoration at this point. He rarely played any music.

That was largely because when he was spending time with Mahiru, the idea of playing music was the last thing on his mind. Listening to Mahiru's voice was much more pleasant.

"What about you guys, Makoto?" Chitose asked.

"I pretty much just listen to whatever's popular…"

"I don't listen to much, but my grandma plays the koto, so I've heard a lot of that."

"That's pretty weird in its own right, though… Which means when it comes to music—Yuuta?" Itsuki suddenly changed the subject. He shot a clearly dissatisfied look at the smiling Yuuta. "Why didn't you tell us you were performing live? If you'd said something, we could have moved our shifts around in advance, ya big jerk."

It sounded like Itsuki had some complaints about Yuuta secretly performing at the culture festival. He pounded firmly on the table as he talked, but not hard enough to spill their drinks.

Makoto seemed bothered by the shaking table, and muttered, "He probably didn't invite you because you'd make such a fuss."

Yuuta just smiled awkwardly in response to Itsuki's complaints. He didn't look apologetic in the least. It seemed like he was used to dealing with it.

"I thought you would do that, and that's why I didn't say anything. I didn't want to make a big thing out of it."

"But Amane and Mahiru saw it! No fair!"

"It's fine, you go to karaoke with me all the time, Itsuki."

"Nuh-uh, I wanted to see you up in the spotlight! There's nothing to do about it now, so I'll forgive you if you give us a solo performance here."

"Wha…?"

Yuuta frowned awkwardly at the unreasonable demand. Then he made eye contact with Amane.

Amane had a bad feeling about it, so he had been averting his eyes as best he could, and now he could see Yuuta grinning at him from across the room.

"All right, I think I'll drag Fujimiya down with me then."

"Why me?!"

"Because it's karaoke, which means singing in front of everyone, right? That doesn't change if we sing together; there's no difference."

"Oh, suddenly we've got more singers for the live show! That's great, the more the merrier."

Itsuki cheered, figuring that Yuuta would sing with more energy if Amane was with him.

Chitose, Ayaka, and the others seemed to be excited as well, and they were shouting enthusiastically, half teasing and half encouraging them.

Amane wasn't enthusiastic about the idea of singing a duet with someone who was a great singer, so he looked at Mahiru, searching for help—

"I don't think I've ever really heard Amane singing before. Now I'm finally getting the chance, so…"

She was clearly on Itsuki's side, so with a shrug of his shoulders, Amane grumbled, "I'll get you guys for this later." And gave in as he reached for the microphone that was lying on the table.

In all the excitement, Amane ended up being pushed into singing many songs by the partygoers around him, and by the time he was done with all the requests, he was worn out.

Yuuta, who had been singing with him, still looked composed. He definitely had better endurance.

"Good job, you were great!"

There was more of a sparkle in Mahiru's eye than usual as she welcomed Amane back to his seat with a gentle smile, so he could tell she was in a party mood, too.

"...You were really getting into it, Mahiru."

"I—I mean...you looked cool while you were singing, so..."

"Thanks for saying so. All right then, you're up next."

"Huh?"

"Chitoseee? I'm lending you Mahiru, so sing something with her next!"

Amane shouted to Chitose, offering his cheerful girlfriend up as the next victim.

Chitose got a suspicious look in her eye when Amane called out to her, but when she heard what he said, she smiled with satisfaction and gave him a happy answer.

"Leave it to me!"

"Wait, what?"

"You enjoyed watching me, so now I want to enjoy hearing you sing."

"Th-that's—"

"If Chitose picks the song, you'll probably know it, too, so there's no problem, no problem at all."

"Y-yes, that's true...Chi-Chitoseee!"

"Come on now, prepare yourself, Mahiru. One way or another, we're all gonna sing and have a good time."

Chitose was all fired up. She pulled Mahiru up by the hand, and Amane waved and watched her go.

Mahiru gave him an angry look, but Amane had already gone down this road, so he thought she should accept it gracefully.

Everything is an experience, he thought keenly, nodding as he gazed at Mahiru being handed a microphone and panicking. He was narrowing his eyes in satisfaction, when Yuuta, who was sitting beside him, picked up a french fry with a wry smile.

"Aren't you worried she's going to get revenge on you later?"

"The most she's going to do is smack me a bunch."

That was a kind of revenge, but it was an adorable revenge, so he would willingly accept it just to see Mahiru's reaction.

Yuuta shrugged at Amane, who was acting unbothered. Then Yuuta stared spellbound up at Mahiru, who had begun singing despite her panic.

Except for swimming, Mahiru could do almost anything well, and singing was no exception. She sounded great. The song that she had chosen, a quiet Japanese number, was just right. The song was extremely pleasant being sung in her clear voice, and everyone stopped chatting to listen.

Amane found himself smiling. Her voice seemed like it would put anyone to sleep if they could get her to sing a lullaby at night.

Chitose was accompanying Mahiru. Her mellow voice sounded good, too.

Actually, given that she was more accustomed to singing, Chitose knew the lyrics better than Mahiru, and her intonation was a better fit for the music. In terms of skill, Chitose was probably the better of the two.

She had a truly satisfied look on her face, and she probably wasn't going to let Mahiru go, even after the song was over.

Well, despite what she said, Mahiru also seems to be enjoying herself, so that wouldn't be so bad.

Even her forsaken, unhappy expression had been replaced by an embarrassed, but gentle smile.

Mahiru, who had apparently never experienced karaoke with a

large group like this, looked like she was enjoying it greatly at the moment, which was also satisfying for Amane.

"...Come to think of it, did you two say you were going home after karaoke?"

As Amane was gazing peacefully at Mahiru holding the microphone, Yuuta, who had come over to sit next to him, whispered a question in a quiet voice that only Amane could hear.

"Yeah. Even with me here, it's dangerous for her to walk outside after it gets too late, and Mahiru has already gotten everything ready for dinner, so we're going."

"Wow, it kind of sounds like you're already living together, seriously."

"Shut up."

Mahiru went back to her own apartment to sleep, change clothes, and use the bath, but otherwise she was pretty much always in Amane's apartment.

The fact that this had become normal for him, and that he didn't feel any discomfort with it, showed just how integrated Mahiru had become into Amane's life.

"So that means that when this karaoke session is over, we'll lose the two of you. Got it. The other folks are probably going to be upset about that, but I guess that's how it's gotta be."

"You mean there are people who will be disappointed that Mahiru's not around, surely."

"Ah-ha-ha, you never think about yourself, do you?"

Smiling wryly, Yuuta prodded Amane in the shoulder, and Amane elbowed him in the side in response, making the point that he was not as big of a presence as Mahiru or Yuuta.

Recently, some of his classmates had been opening up to him, but that didn't mean that he was as popular as the two of them, and if anyone regretted his absence, he was sure it would only be because he was part of a set with Mahiru.

For some reason, their classmates had been warmly watching over them, and he had a feeling that was the cause.

"That's because in a way, you're treated like a set, to the point where if someone mentions Fujimiya, they just naturally end up talking about Miss Shiina, too. But I think there are quite a few people in our class who also like you for your personality, Fujimiya. Once people talk to you, they see that you're surprisingly approachable and very kind."

"I'm glad to hear there are people who think so highly of me. But, for today, we're just going to go home."

"Ah-ha-ha, if your plans are already set, then there's no helping it. But I hope you have another chance to hang out and have fun with everybody from class."

"Yeah, me too."

Even Amane, who wasn't particularly good at hanging out with other people, felt that it was important to build connections with his classmates like this after making it through the culture festival, and he'd had fun doing it, too.

Still, he wouldn't want it to become a frequent thing. But occasionally doing something for fun with their classmates wasn't so bad. The fact that he had come around to thinking that way was probably one of the greatest returns on his investment in this culture festival.

Even he was amazed by his attitude, which would have been unthinkable just a year earlier. Feeling tickled by this realization, Amane smiled gently back at Yuuta, who was smiling at him.

"Hey, so, Amane?"

Amane had finished his drink and was standing in front of the drink bar wondering what to have next, when Itsuki came up and addressed him in a somewhat stiff tone of voice.

His voice was quiet enough that it was nearly drowned out by the music playing in the karaoke studio, but Amane could hear him perfectly clearly, and he sensed that Itsuki's expression was tense.

"What's up?"

The difference in Itsuki's demeanor from a moment earlier when he had been cheerfully livening the place up told Amane what he was about to ask, but even so, Amane deliberately answered no differently than he usually would.

"Listen man, today, after I took Chi away, what did you talk about with my dad?"

"...It's kind of hard to say exactly. He didn't really say anything bad about you two or anything. He just met my parents and then we chatted a little, that's all."

"Yeah? Here I was thinking that my dad definitely said something weird."

"You don't have much faith in your father, do you? ...I don't really know how to put this, but I don't think he did anything that you should be worried about."

As he filled his cup with rattling ice cubes, Amane affected a gentle tone, trying his best not to put any unnecessary emotion into his voice.

If he fussed over it too much, Itsuki would just laugh and hide everything away, so Amane stubbornly maintained a certain level of distance, having no choice but to address things in a flat tone.

Trying his best not to seem too concerned, Amane pushed the button for melon soda, filling his transparent cup with a vivid green. The clinking noise of the ice and the sound of fizzing bubbles did a little to relieve the heavy silence that had fallen over them.

Realizing that his melon soda, which he had filled to the brim, might spill before he got it back to the room, Amane slowly brought the cup to his lips and drank a little. It was refreshing and sweet, and as he sipped it, it tickled his throat. He narrowed his eyes a little at the sensation, then smiled at Itsuki, who was standing there silently.

"Well, when it comes to your situation at home, and the bad blood between Chitose and your father...what I mean is, I don't know exactly what made him reject her like that. But I do think it's better for the two of you to be together, it just wouldn't feel right if you weren't... I get the feeling that you wouldn't make it without Chitose, and I hope that everything goes right for you two. I can't imagine the two of you ever being apart."

He wasn't sure if the cold feeling of the drink going down his throat was helping him keep his cool, but he was aware that he was being uncharacteristically encouraging, and he felt his cheeks heat up a little. However, he felt like he had to say at least that much, so he had gone ahead and said it.

After quietly listening to Amane talk, Itsuki screwed his face up like he was about to cry for a second, then put on a smile that was both impish and bashful, to try to hide it.

"What's with you?"

"Nothing, it's just, like, kinda embarrassing."

"Well, who made me say it?"

"Bwa-ha-ha, me, I guess. It's because I started such a bummer of a conversation."

Amane didn't say a thing about the expression that had crossed Itsuki's face a second earlier, he just made a jab at his friend like always, keeping things light. Itsuki seemed relieved.

As soon as Amane had noticed that Itsuki didn't have an empty cup in his hand, he'd figured out that he'd come to the drink bar to talk to him.

Empty-handed, Itsuki leaned against the studio wall, and Amane stood next to him rattling his cup.

After all, the girls were sure to be having fun for a while. It wouldn't cause any trouble if Amane and Itsuki were gone for a little bit.

After a brief silence, Itsuki slowly opened his mouth. "…I more or less know what my dad wanted to say, you know? And I also know the reason why he hates Chi."

Amane had been listening to the music faintly spilling out from the other rooms as he waited quietly for Itsuki to speak.

"Is it something that I can ask you about?"

"Oh, I can tell you."

"Okay."

Amane was glad that he wasn't going to have to pry for an explanation.

Itsuki looked at him in amusement, smiled and shrugged. "I'm just guessing now, but I think the reason dad hates Chi has something to do with my brother."

"Oh yeah, you've got an older brother, don't you?"

Itsuki didn't like to talk about his own family much. However, Amane had heard that he had an adult older brother, and that the two of them didn't get along.

"Sure do. He's eight years older than me, so he's already an adult. For better or worse, he's nothing like me. He's serious, and straightforward, and sincere, and he was my father's pride and joy."

"…Was?"

"I entered my rebellious phase early, but he had his after he was an adult, you see."

Itsuki told him this frankly, and without emotion, and yet there was a smile in his voice. He looked at Amane and asked, "You must have had some idea, Amane?"

Itsuki continued, "My family lineage is, well, as you've guessed, it's a pretty notable bloodline. Meaning that my father gave us a real proper upbringing, so that we wouldn't bring shame to the family."

"...From what I've heard about how you were raised in the past, I assumed your brother got the same treatment."

"Except he was even stricter with my brother than he was with me. My brother got saddled with the expectation that he would be the family heir, and he was raised with that in mind. It suited my brother's nature just fine, and at the time, he apparently didn't have any reservations about it."

Itsuki claimed that his older brother had originally been a levelheaded, serious, diligent person. Then he let Amane see a hint of a sour smile.

"But, once he grew up and went out into the world, one day he realized something. He wondered why he was living such a regimented life, and why he didn't get to do anything he want to do, ya know?"

"And?"

"I don't think that everything our father did while raising us was wrong, and I know that he cares for us in his own way. And I think that he really doted on me and my brother, much more than our workaholic mother, who was really distant and basically never paid attention to anything we did."

It certainly seemed like Itsuki had hardly ever seen his mother, since he never really talked about her much. But as far as Amane had seen, Itsuki's father cared about his son and was trying to have a relationship with him.

"Even so, my brother realized that he was just following the path that our parents had decided for him, and that he had never decided a single thing for himself. Around that time, he met someone he liked... Well, she's his wife now, but anyway, he met that person, and for the first time, my brother defied my father. 'I'm marrying this woman! If you don't approve, I won't be your successor!' he said."

"...And I'm guessing that this brother of yours is now...?"

Amane realized that although he had been aware that Itsuki had an older brother, he had never actually seen him at the Akazawa house. But now that he thought about it, it was strange that the oldest son was never there if he was supposed to inherit the place.

"Right, right. After all these twists and turns, my brother and his wife live somewhere else, for now. They left while I was in middle school. Tentatively, for now at least, my brother has agreed to be my father's heir, and my brother and his wife are living separately until I'm an adult and can leave the house. But no one knows when he might change his mind, so dad is always anxious about it. And so—I'm backing up here—but when the time comes, if my brother refuses to inherit the estate, then it becomes a question of what Dad will do. The first choice is obviously gonna be to push the burden down to his second son."

Itsuki's tone told Amane that he found the whole thing bothersome. But even Amane could have predicted how things would turn out.

Somebody had to inherit the family estate that had been passed down for generation after generation, so if the eldest son wouldn't take it, and there was a second son, the natural course of events was that that second son would be selected as the heir.

"Even though we were always disciplined more strictly than other kids, dad put even more intense pressure on my brother about this one thing. And until I met Chi, I'll say this about myself now, I felt like I had to be some top-rate honor student and all-around goody-two-shoes."

"…I can't even imagine."

"Compared to how I am now, I was a totally different guy."

Itsuki was smiling foolishly, but Amane also knew that at heart, he was an honest person.

Itsuki acted the way that he did on purpose. Amane knew that his friend was brilliant enough to do most anything if he put his mind to it, but the version of Itsuki that other people saw was a laid-back, freewheeling, optimistic person. And Itsuki himself was pleased with how he conducted himself these days and wasn't inclined to change.

"Well, once I met Chi, I entered my rebellious phase, just like my brother, and that sent my dad into a panic once he realized his predicament."

"...Because if you leave, too, then the family line is in danger, right?"

"Right, exactly. And on top of that, well...when she came to meet my father, I mean, she was the same Chi that you know now. It was like she reminded him of my brother's wife in some way, and...that, he said, he could never accept."

From Daiki's point of view, his second son's new girlfriend resembled the woman who had swept in and turned his favored eldest son away from the proper path. It probably felt almost like a kind of trauma from his perspective.

Amane could understand how that would be difficult for Daiki to accept. But that didn't make it okay for him to equate the two.

"So, that's one of the major reasons why Dad can't accept Chi. And the other one is...because I got hurt standing up for her, probably."

"...You got hurt?"

"Yeah, I bet Yuuta and them didn't tell you anything about this. Even I don't talk about it, because I don't want Chi to feel guilty. Ah, you don't have to worry about it, okay? It wasn't a serious injury or anything."

Itsuki was purposefully keeping a mild demeanor as he talked, so that he wouldn't upset Amane. He gave an exaggerated shrug to express his exasperation.

"Yeah, I think you know about all the stuff that happened with the fighting in the track and field club, and that upperclassman in the club falling for me. But later, after me and Chi started dating, that same upperclassman came after Chi again. I saw her take a swing, and I didn't want Chi to get hurt again, so I stepped in and, well, I kinda wound up being the one who got hurt instead."

Itsuki was speaking in a lighthearted tone, but Amane couldn't help but feel that it was a pretty outrageous way to get involved. But still, it sounded like, to Itsuki, it was all in the past, and he maintained his lighthearted smile.

"It really wasn't that bad of an injury, but since it happened at school, you know, it became a whole thing and they had to call my parents. So my dad found out about it, and it cemented his attitude toward Chi even more… He saw her as the cause of a lot of unnecessary trouble for his son."

There was something faintly bitter in Itsuki's voice as he said this last part, but his lighthearted tone didn't change, which made it all the more evident how resentful and worried he was. The more personal something was, the harder Itsuki tried not to show any weakness to others.

As far as Amane had heard, it frankly didn't seem like this was something Chitose could have done anything about.

Sure, it was obvious that Daiki and Chitose had somewhat incompatible personalities, but the other cause of their conflict was much larger.

Chitose had gotten caught up in the antagonism between Daiki, Itsuki's older brother, and his older brother's wife. Then someone had committed an act of jealousy against Chitose, a crime that she couldn't have done anything to prevent.

Amane didn't blame Chitose for trying, but no amount of effort could turn things around unless they dealt with the underlying issue.

"So it's not a question of Chi not trying hard enough; not really, I don't think. Sure, it's true that Chi has never measured up in my dad's eyes, but it goes without saying that he and I are really to blame. The only reason we're in this mess is because I've been doing what I want without actually facing up to my father."

"Have you talked to Chitose about this?"

"Nope. What I just told you is all my own speculation, but even so, I can't explain that to Chi. Even setting aside the thing about her being compared to my brother's wife, if I dug up the injury thing again, it would definitely hurt her. She'd say it was because of her. That it was her fault... I don't wanna hear her say those things."

"...Ah."

"Chi's not to blame. So, I can't accept the way my dad treats her. Me getting hurt was my responsibility, it had nothing to do with her. I just didn't follow through, that's all. I didn't beat the snot out of that upperclassman... I wonder if I should have done something, for her sake."

Itsuki seemed to spit that last part out, releasing a lot of pent-up emotion. But then he looked Amane in the eye and said, "Don't look so worried man." And flashed one of his usual droll smiles. "Anyway, keep this a secret, would you? Though I don't guess you wouldn't want to do anything that might make Chi stop smiling, either."

"Of course not."

"Mm-hmm. That's why you're my best friend, Amane."

In a way, Itsuki was forcing himself to act cheerful, and Amane chuckled quietly and accepted his words.

"What, you're not gonna argue?" Itsuki prodded.

"...Do you want me to?"

"Aw, c'mon, don't say that. I'll go ahead and gladly take your silence to mean that you agree."

"Well, I definitely didn't agree..."

"Would you quit yankin' me around?! Come on, pal!"

"Shut up. Don't shout right in my ear."

"Lame!"

They didn't want to go back to the party room in a gloomy mood, so Itsuki found his typical raucous voice and cheerful face, and Amane fell back into his own serious demeanor again. It was like nothing had happened, despite what they had shared.

Amane silently marveled at the way that Itsuki could instantly make it look like he wasn't hiding a thing. Amane also chuckled as if nothing was out of the ordinary, and followed his friend back to the room where everyone else was partying.

By then, his melon soda was already flat, but nobody noticed.

Chapter 14

The Angel's Request

Even after hearing Itsuki's story, Amane sang along and chatted casually with everyone just as before, and before he knew it, it was time to go.

After karaoke, the other partygoers decided to go eat dinner at a casual restaurant, but Amane and Mahiru were splitting off from the group. Everyone was reluctant to let them leave, and even Amane felt a little sad to go, but it would have been terrible if anything happened to Mahiru, so they headed home.

From serving customers at the culture festival, to cleanup afterward, and then a party after that, the day had been one event after another, so his body was pretty tired, but the fact that he still wasn't completely fatigued was probably because he had been training his body with exercise. He still had a spring in his step by the time they made it home.

"Ah, I'm wiped out."

"Heh-heh, you worked hard."

They ate the simple dinner that Mahiru had prepared for them that day and settled in to relax.

It could have been that both of them were feeling slightly mentally drained from waiting on customers, but Mahiru's smile seemed more subdued than usual. It wasn't that it lacked brilliance, only that there seemed to be less energy in her smile than usual.

Amane was concerned that she also seemed to be feeling a little awkward.

"...Is something bothering you?"

"Huh?"

"Ah, you just don't really seem yourself. I was worried that something unpleasant or troubling might have happened today at the culture festival."

"N-no...troubling? Not really."

"That's not a very convincing denial."

"Well, there was that thing the first day..."

"...Sorry, for making you remember that."

"Ah, n-no that's not what I meant! ...Troubled...I guess you could say...right now, there is something on my mind."

Amane didn't worry that he was being rejected or unwanted because he was talking to Mahiru, and he didn't know what she was worried about yet.

No matter how close Amane and Mahiru were, without words, they could not really communicate. That was precisely why they had decided between themselves to always listen to what the other had to say. But even though Mahiru must have remembered that agreement, she seemed to be having a hard time speaking. She kept moving her lips as she struggled with the words.

From the way she was acting, Amane assumed that he must be the cause, and that she must be unhappy with him, and yet she didn't seem like she was blaming him for anything.

He stared straight into her slightly wavering caramel-colored eyes wondering what on earth was the matter. Eventually, Mahiru parted her lips slightly, and it seemed like she was ready to talk.

"…I…I said that I had some things I needed to talk to you about after the culture festival was over, didn't I?"

"Hmm? Ah, right, you did say that."

"So the thing is…I'm not really sure how to say this. Amane, well, this might be the wrong way to put this, but I'm the only one you think of, right?"

"Yeah."

"And you don't have any interest in other girls, do you?"

"What? Of course not…"

Obviously it would be a problem if he was checking out other girls, despite having a girlfriend.

"Well, that makes me incredibly happy, and I also think it's one of your virtues, Amane. But because you only have eyes for me… you're probably indifferent to the attention you're getting from other girls."

"I think they're just wondering how someone like me ended up with someone like you."

"…They like *you*, Amane, and you're not paying attention, so you don't even notice."

Amane blinked dramatically at her totally unexpected words, and a slightly bitter smile appeared on Mahiru's lips.

"Earlier, at karaoke, when I went to the bathroom, I just happened to overhear some classmates talking about how great you were. The same thing happened during the culture festival. You looked so cool, and even the customers were complimenting you."

"I never really noticed any of that stuff. Are you sure?"

"Yes… I'm happy that other people are finally recognizing your charm… At the same time, I hate the idea that my Amane, the Amane that only I know, is disappearing. Along with the assumption that I'm the only one you might be interested in."

In short, Mahiru had been feeling the very same emotion that he had been feeling toward her. The nature of it was a little different, but basically, she was jealous.

"The culture festival is over, so please let me say this. I really...I kind of hated seeing you smiling at customers, looking as cool as you did. You're supposed to be all mine."

Mahiru made her best effort to say what she had to say, in a slightly faltering tone of voice, and embraced him, emphasizing the point that he belonged to her.

He knew he shouldn't laugh at her confession of jealousy and possessiveness, but a smile automatically rose to his lips.

...*She really loves me, huh.*

He had once again glimpsed the endlessly pure and vast well of affection that Mahiru had for him, and he knew that he also felt the same for her. It made him a little self-conscious.

Although she showed a slight bit of hesitation, Mahiru didn't give up and clung tightly to Amane. He used his opposite arm, the one she wasn't holding onto, to stroke her head.

"Rest assured, please. There are plenty of things that everyone else doesn't know about me, and the only one who'll get to discover them is you, Mahiru... For starters, did you know that I'm a more jealous guy than you thought?"

Mahiru hadn't really experienced it yet, but Amane's feelings of jealousy could be very strong.

Showing his jealousy openly wasn't really in Amane's nature. He was too immature, and Mahiru's popularity was common knowledge and not something that he could try to change, so he had resigned himself to it. He also understood perfectly well that Mahiru's attention wasn't wandering or anything.

That said, he still didn't find it very pleasant, and if he could, he would've had her always stay in arm's reach.

"These past two days, with so many eyes on you, I've been so jealous, I've been thinking that I don't want to be apart from you."

"...Yeah."

"You're the only one I see, Mahiru... I'm already yours and yours alone, so hog me all you want. And I'll keep you all to myself, too."

As if to get back all the time they had lost to the culture festival, Mahiru snuggled up next to Amane, and he put his arms around her and wrapped her whole dainty body in his embrace. After stiffening for just a moment, Mahiru entrusted everything to him, and leaned against Amane.

She was no longer a maid who smiled at everyone. She was just a regular girl, showing him the special smile that was meant for him alone.

Mahiru's eyes were sweet and full of trust as she peered up at him. Amane smiled at her utterly straightforward affection, and in order to ease any worries that she was still holding, he stole a kiss from her anxious lips.

Her lips were just as sweet as her eyes, and he felt himself melt into them ever so gently. Mahiru happily closed her eyes and accepted Amane's delicate kiss.

He wanted to cherish his time with Mahiru as much as humanly possible and didn't kiss her too deeply, keeping it light and sweet. They were kissing each other, which was just enough to feel each other's heat. When Amane stopped, he rubbed Mahiru's back in a comforting way. She drew her lips away slowly and reluctantly.

Her eyes, flooded with tears, but harboring a quiet and loving— yet expectant and greedy—look, lingered on Amane with some embarrassment.

He didn't understand the meaning behind her look, and before

©Hanekoto

he could ask her what the matter was, Mahiru buried her face in Amane's arms and seemed to be hunting for something with her slim fingers.

Timidly, she gripped his shirt, and in his arms, he heard her whisper quietly, "…Today…is it all right…if I don't go home?"

Afterword

Thank you so much for picking up this book.

I am the author, Saekisan. I trust that you enjoyed Volume 7 of *The Angel Next Door*?

I mean…they were in maid costumes—Mahiru was a maid. If you're reading the afterword, I assume that you have finished looking through the book, so you already know about maid Mahiru.

This was the culture festival volume, so of course having the kids run a café was a sure hit, and having them dress up as maids was sure to suit Mahiru. She's so cute. The classical maid look is just the best.

In this volume, Mahiru is feeling secretly jealous while watching Amane spread his wings, but in the end, she can't suppress how she feels. Both of them can be reserved, but they're gradually becoming bolder, aren't they? In this volume, Mahiru is the more assertive one. Who put that idea into her head? (feigns ignorance)

And so we find Amane struggling with his self-control. It'll be interesting to see how long he can hold out.

At the end of this volume Mahiru said something explosive, but you'll have to see how it turns out in the next book.

*　　*　　*

Once again, we got Hanekoto to draw some splendid illustrations for this book. They're really great—like, whooooaaah!

I pretty much leave the composition of the illustrations up to Hanekoto, and every single time I get something outstanding. The pinup-style frontispiece is beyond magnificent. (I can't find the words)

Since Volume 7 was the culture festival volume, we got an illustration of Mahiru getting ready, but the thing is, why does it look so erotic? My eyes must be wicked, I guess.

By the way, I love all the illustrations, but personally, the one I really, really love this time—my number one picture—is Mahiru looking embarrassed. Why is she so cute?

Now we've reached the end, but I need to thank everyone who has helped me.

To the head editor who worked so hard to get this book published, to everyone in the editing department at GA Books, to everyone in the sales department, to the proofreaders, to Hanekoto, to everyone in the print shop, and to all of you who picked up a copy; truly, thank you so much.

Let's meet again in the next volume.

Thank you very much for reading to the end!

HAVE YOU BEEN TURNED ON TO LIGHT NOVELS YET?

86—EIGHTY-SIX, VOL. 1-12

In truth, there is no such thing as a bloodless war. Beyond the fortified walls protecting the eighty-five Republic Sectors lies the "nonexistent" Eighty-Sixth Sector. The young men and women of this forsaken land are branded the Eighty-Six and, stripped of their humanity, pilot "unmanned" weapons into battle...

Manga adaptation available now!

WOLF & PARCHMENT, VOL. 1-8

The young man Col dreams of one day joining the holy clergy and departs on a journey from the bathhouse, Spice and Wolf. Winfiel Kingdom's prince has invited him to help correct the sins of the Church. But as his travels begin, Col discovers in his luggage a young girl with a wolf's ears and tail named Myuri, who stowed away for the ride!

Manga adaptation available now!

SOLO LEVELING, VOL. 1-8

E-rank hunter Jinwoo Sung has no money, no talent, and no prospects to speak of—and apparently, no luck, either! When he enters a hidden double dungeon one fateful day, he's abandoned by his party and left to die at the hands of some of the most horrific monsters he's ever encountered.

Comic adaptation available now!